DREAMWORKS

Trolls #4

"Brain Freeze"

PAPERCUTZ

NEW YORK

MORE GREAT GRAPHIC NOVEL SERIES AVAILABLE FROM PAPERCUTZ

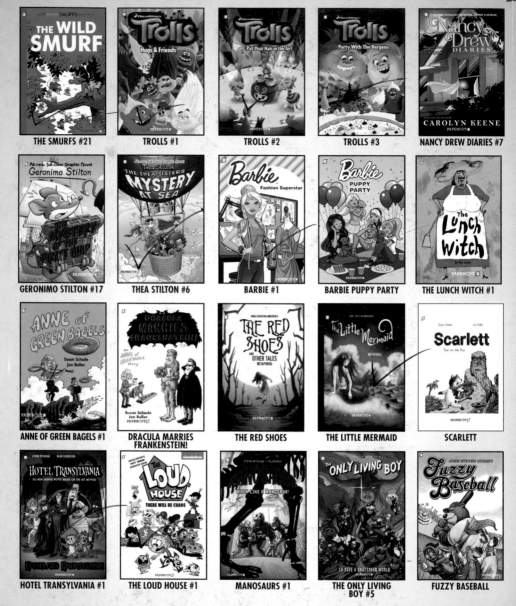

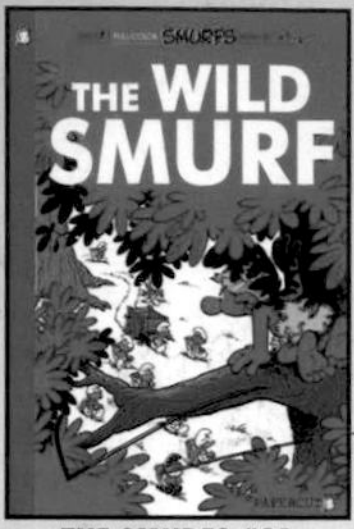
THE WILD SMURF
PAPERCUTZ
THE SMURFS #21

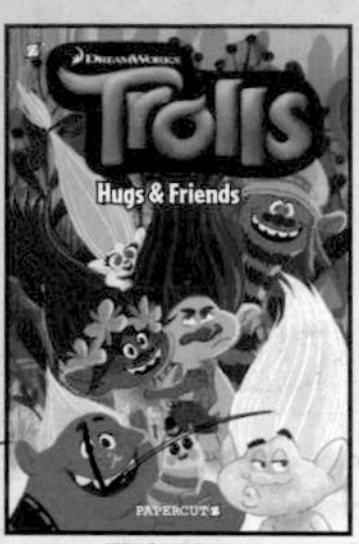
DreamWorks
Trolls
Hugs & Friends
PAPERCUTZ
TROLLS #1

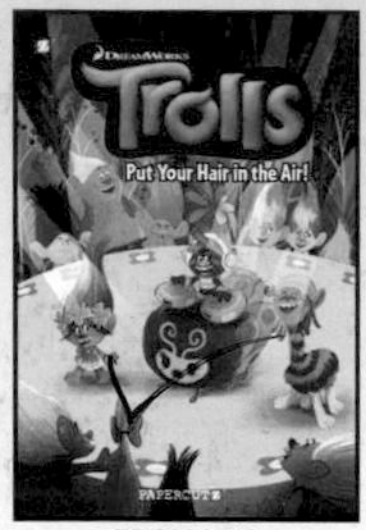
DreamWorks
Trolls
Put Your Hair in the Air!
PAPERCUTZ
TROLLS #2

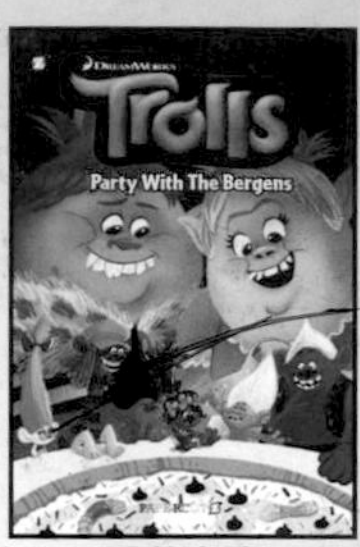
DreamWorks
Trolls
Party With The Bergens
TROLLS #3

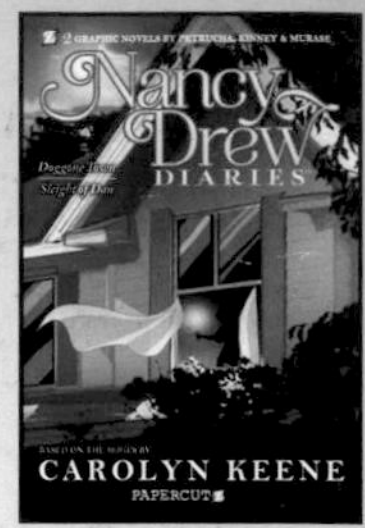
Nancy Drew
DIARIES
CAROLYN KEENE
PAPERCUTZ
NANCY DREW DIARIES #7

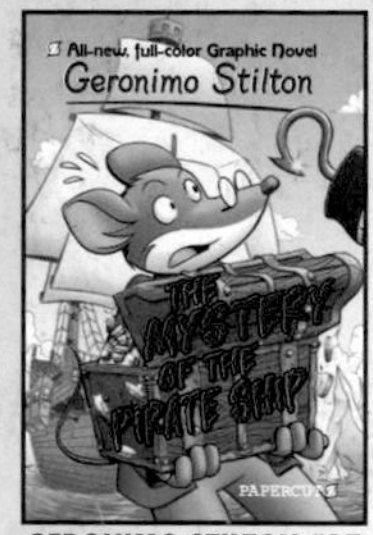
All-new, full-color Graphic Novel
Geronimo Stilton
THE MYSTERY OF THE PIRATE SHIP
PAPERCUTZ
GERONIMO STILTON #17

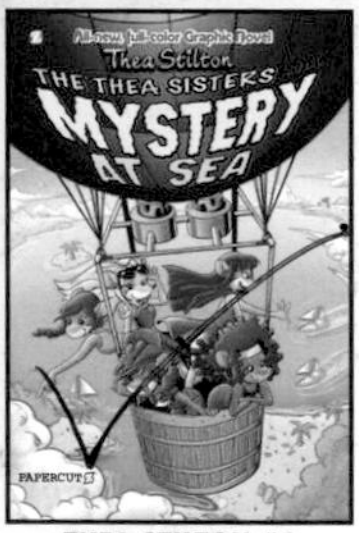
All-new, full-color Graphic Novel
Thea Stilton
THE THEA SISTERS
MYSTERY AT SEA
PAPERCUTZ
THEA STILTON #6

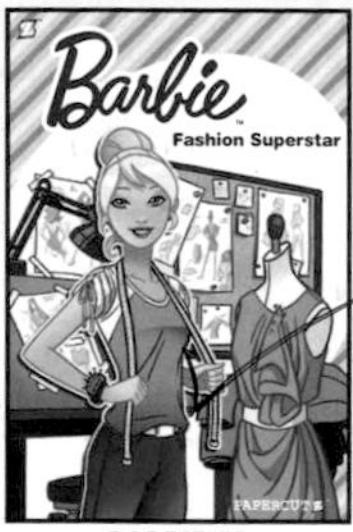
Barbie
Fashion Superstar
PAPERCUTZ
BARBIE #1

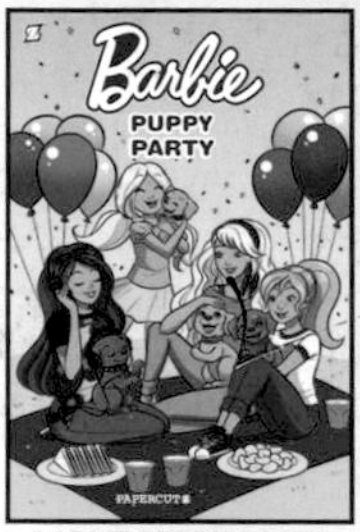
Barbie
PUPPY PARTY
PAPERCUTZ
BARBIE PUPPY PARTY

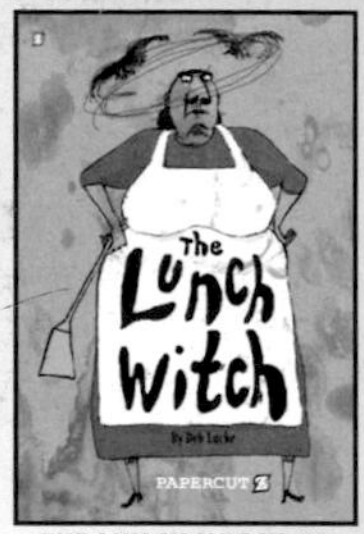
The Lunch Witch
PAPERCUTZ
THE LUNCH WITCH #1

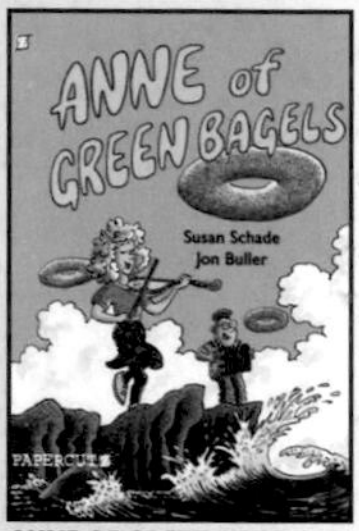
ANNE of GREEN BAGELS
Susan Schade
Jon Buller
PAPERCUTZ
ANNE OF GREEN BAGELS #1

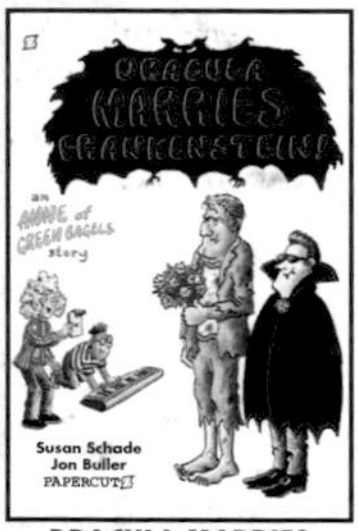
DRACULA MARRIES FRANKENSTEIN!
an ANNE of GREEN BAGELS story
Susan Schade
Jon Buller
PAPERCUTZ
DRACULA MARRIES FRANKENSTEIN!

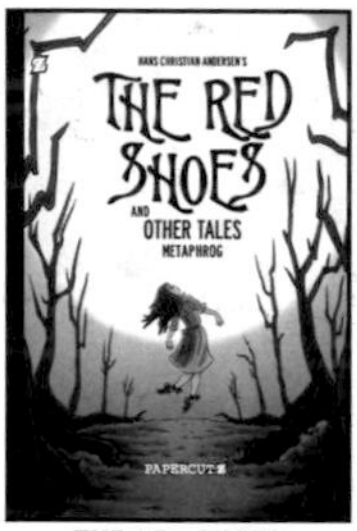
HANS CHRISTIAN ANDERSEN'S
THE RED SHOES
AND OTHER TALES
METAPHROG
PAPERCUTZ
THE RED SHOES

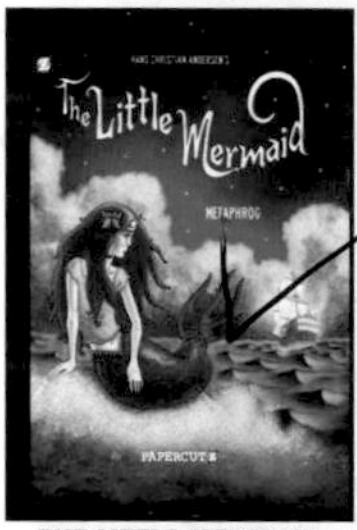
HANS CHRISTIAN ANDERSEN'S
The Little Mermaid
METAPHROG
PAPERCUTZ
THE LITTLE MERMAID

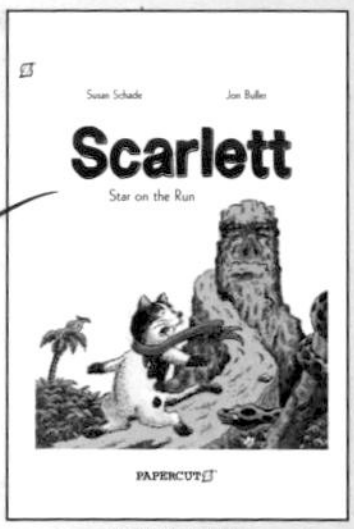
Susan Schade
Jon Buller
Scarlett
Star on the Run
PAPERCUTZ
SCARLETT

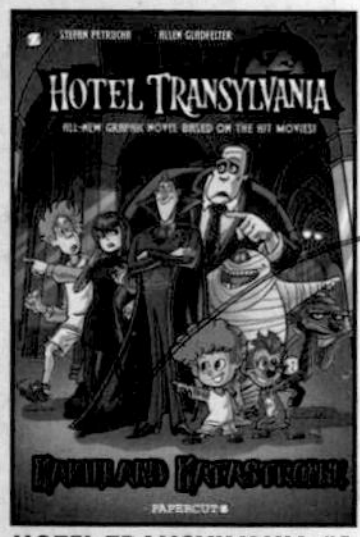
HOTEL TRANSYLVANIA
PAPERCUTZ
HOTEL TRANSYLVANIA #1

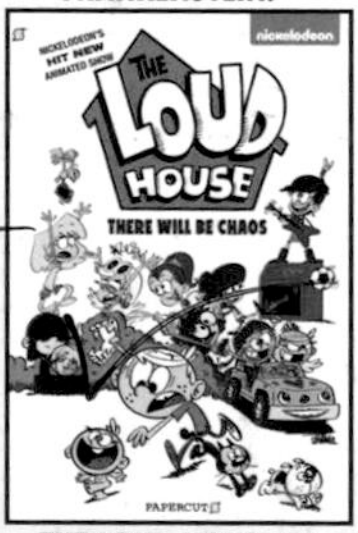
nickelodeon
THE LOUD HOUSE
THERE WILL BE CHAOS
PAPERCUTZ
THE LOUD HOUSE #1

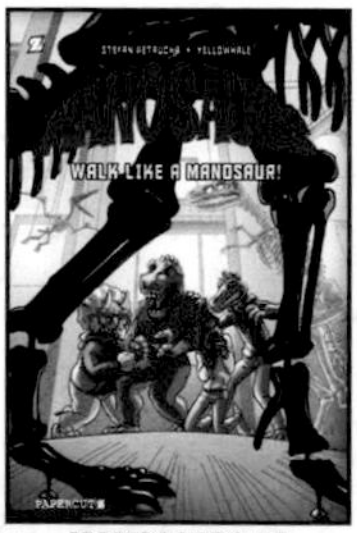
WALK LIKE A MANOSAUR!
PAPERCUTZ
MANOSAURS #1

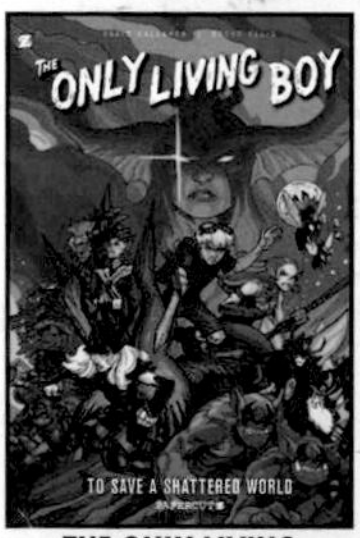
THE ONLY LIVING BOY
TO SAVE A SHATTERED WORLD
PAPERCUTZ
THE ONLY LIVING BOY #5

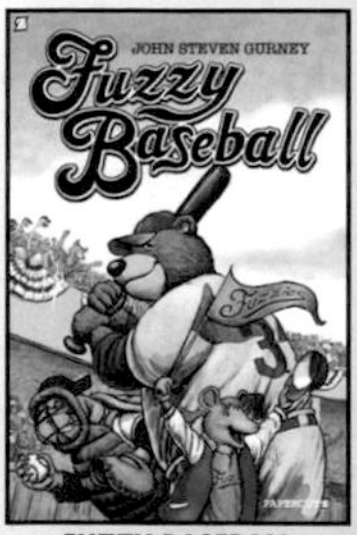
JOHN STEVEN GURNEY
Fuzzy Baseball
PAPERCUTZ
FUZZY BASEBALL

THE SMURFS, BARBIE, HOTEL TRANSYLVANIA, MANOSAURS, THE LOUD HOUSE and TROLLS graphic novels are available for $7.9 in paperback, and $12.99 in hardcover. THE ONLY LIVING BOY graphic novels are available for $8.99 in paperback, and $13.99 hardcover. GERONIMO STILTON and THEA STILTON graphic novels are available for $9.99 in hardcover only. FUZZY BASEBALL and NANCY DREW DIARIES graphic novels are available for $9.99 in paperback only. THE LUNCH WITCH, SCARLETT, and ANNE OF GREEN BAGELS graphic novels are available for $14.99 in paperback only. THE RED SHOES and THE LITTLE MERMAID graphic nove are available for $12.99 in hardcover only. DRACULA MARRIES FRANKENSTEIN! graphic novel is available for $12.99 in paperback onl

Available from booksellers everywhere. You can also order online from www.papercutz.com. Or call 1-800-886-1223, Monday through Frida 9–5 EST. MC, Visa, and AmEx accepted. To order by mail, please add $5.00 for postage and handling for first book ordered, $1.00 for eac additional book and make check payable to NBM Publishing. Send to: Papercutz, 160 Broadway, Suite 700, East Wing, New York, NY 1003

THE SMURFS, THE LOUD HOUSE, THE ONLY LIVING BOY, BARBIE, TROLLS, GERONIMO STILTON, THEA STILTON, FUZZY BASEBALL THE LUNCH WITCH, THE LITTLE MERMAID, HOTEL TRANSYLVANIA, MANOSAURS, THE RED SHOES, NANCY DREW DIARIES, ANNE OF GREEN BAGELS, and SCARLETT graphic novels are also available wherever e-books are sold.

TABLE OF CONTENTS

#4 TROLLS

"Brain Freeze"

"BRAIN FREEZE"
Script: Dave Scheidt
Art and Colors: Kathryn Hudson
Letters: Wilson Ramos Jr.

"WATCH OUT FOR HUGS"
Script: Rafał Skarżycki
Art: Miguel Fernandez
Colors: Artful Doodlers
Letters: Dawn Guzzo
Edits: Barry Hutchinson

"NEW FRIENDS"
Script: Dave Scheidt
Art and Colors: Kathryn Hudson
Letters: Wilson Ramos Jr.

"MR. DINK-ILL"
Script: Rafał Skarżycki and Barry Hutchinson
Art and Colors: Monika Nikodem
Letters: Dawn Guzzo

"RAP BATTLE"
Script: Dave Scheidt
Art and Colors: Kathryn Hudson
Letters: Wilson Ramos Jr.

"HAPPY CRITTER DAY"
Script: Dave Scheidt
Art and Colors: Kathryn Hudson
Letters: Wilson Ramos Jr.

"ALONG CAME A SPIDER"
Script: Michał Gałek
Art: Miguel Fernandez
Colors: Monika Nikodem
Letters: Dawn Guzzo

Production — Dawn K. Guzzo
Editor — Robert V. Conte
Assistant Managing Editor — Jeff Whitman
Jim Salicrup
Editor-in-Chief

Special Thanks to DreamWorks Animation LLC —
Corinne Combs, Lawrence "Shifty" Hamashima, Mike
Sund, Barbara Layman, Alex Ward, John Tanzer, and
Megan Startz

ISBN: 978-1-62991-830-3 Paperback Edition
ISBN: 978-1-62991-831-0 Hardcover Edition

Printed in China November 2017

Papercutz books may be purchased for business or promotional use. For
information on bulk purchases please contact Macmillan Corporate and
Premium Sales Department at (800) 221-7945 x5442.

Distributed by Macmillan
First Printing

MEET MORE Trolls

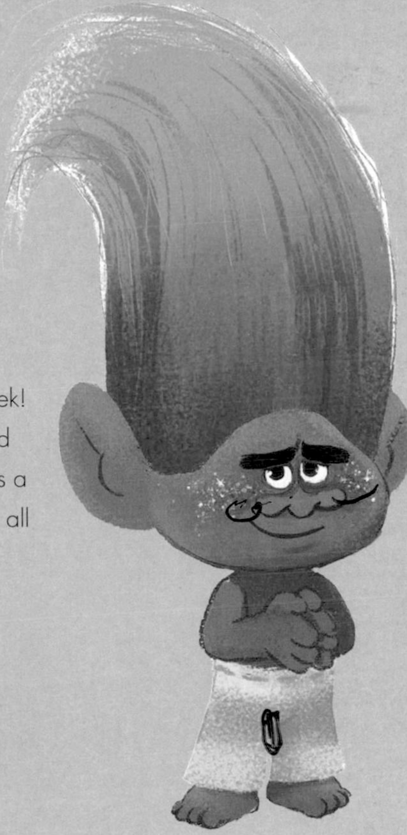

CREEK

He's calm, collected and capable—he's Creek! Positive, supportive and reassuring as a friend and dance partner, Creek is what's known as a Troll's Troll— all the guys want to be him, and all the girls want to be with him!

FUN FACTS

- Always knows what to say to cheer up others
- His freckles are made of glitter
- When he sings, other Trolls listen
- Somehow always manages to steal the spotlight and be the center of attention

FUZZBERT

An enigma wrapped in a riddle, Fuzzbert is a Troll that's made entirely of hair—only his two feet are visible beneath a tuft of bright green Troll hair. Sort of like the "Cousin It" of Troll Village, he communicates with the other Trolls using Wookie-like guttural noises (which they all seem to be able to understand just fine).

FUN FACTS

- Really hard to hear under all of that hair
- Hair shakes when Fuzzbert laughs
- Nicknamed "Twinkle Toes" when dancing
- Uses entire body to tickle other Trolls

MEET MORE Trolls

BABY POPPY

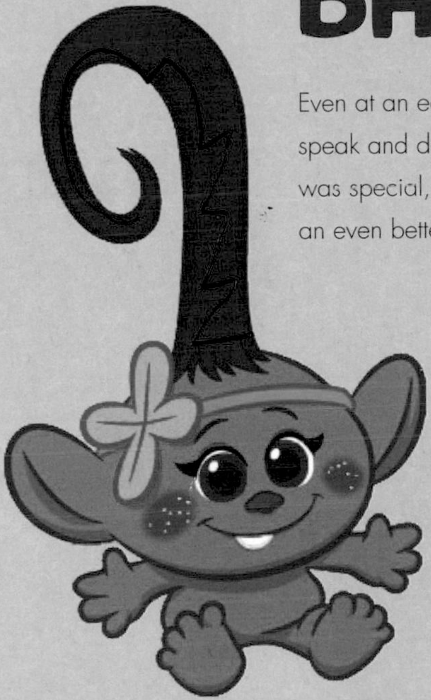

Even at an early age, Baby Poppy wanted to sing before she could speak and dance before she could crawl! Knowing that his daughter was special, King Peppy raised Poppy to be a great leader...and an even better person.

FUN FACTS

- Used her Dad's hair as a playpen
- Childhood friends with the other members of the Snack Pack
- Her first word was "Cowbell"
- Has been hosting rockin' parties ever since she turned one

KARMA

Karma gives new meaning to the word "organic"! She lives in a greenhouse which in Troll Village is more of a rainbow house! Feeling happiest when frolicking in nature, Karma loves climbing trees, building camping gear out of flocked leaves, and befriending all of the huggable caterbugs that like to nap in her hair!

FUN FACTS

- Troll Village's best climber and tunneler
- Loves the feel of Troll Village's enchanted soil between her toes
- Expert whittler and leaf-working specialist
- Mimics the calls of all of the forest's many huggable caterbugs

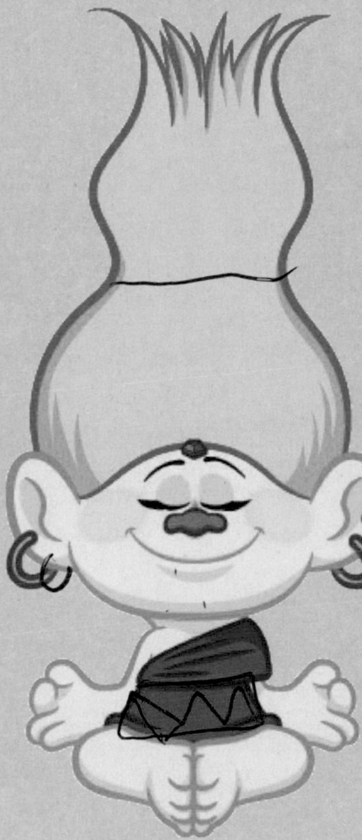

CYBIL

As Troll Village's appointed life coach, Cybil shares obviously simple wisdom with anyone who will listen. Her favorite proverbs are "Only a light can brighten the darkness" and "A door is just a barrier to the next room." Hang around Cybil long enough, and soon you'll be coasting on a gentle wave of harmony!

FUN FACTS

- So "in the moment" that she can forget conversations from one minute ago
- Rides that gentle wave of harmony to float on a cushion of Troll wisdom
- Great listener who loves to give advice
- When she's happy, Cybil dances on air—literally!

MEET MORE TROLLS

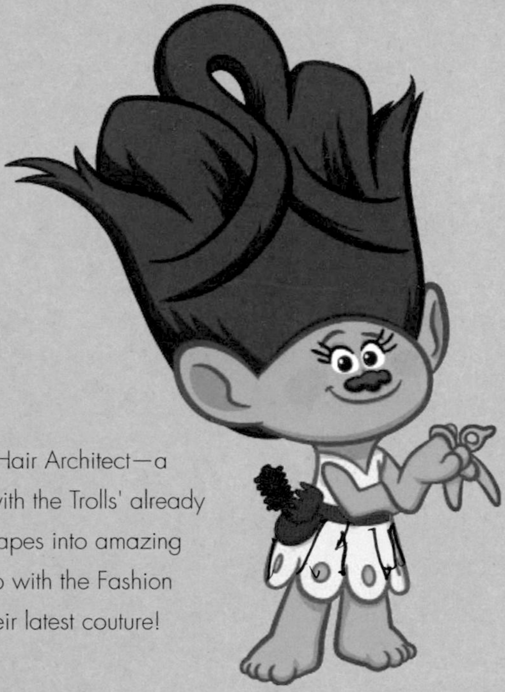

MADDY

Maddy isn't just a hair stylist, she's a Hair Architect—a glamour designer working wonders with the Trolls' already magical hair, which she styles and shapes into amazing new creations. Maddy often teams up with the Fashion Twins, pairing her trendy 'dos with their latest couture!

FUN FACTS

- Runs Troll Village's local hair salon
- Loves to gossip
- Favorite part of her job: Helping others let their true colors shine
- Can double anyone's height with Troll hair extensions

CHEF

Chef likes Trolls. She likes them drenched in butter, she likes them spread on toast, and during Trollstice she makes an excellent Troll meatloaf! But all of that deflated like a bad Troll soufflé the day the Trolls escaped. Now, after wandering the forest in exile, Chef has started cooking up a new recipe to bring Trolls back to Bergen Town.

FUN FACTS

- Impatient and gruff
- Loves to whack underlings with her ladle
- Has many Troll recipes, like Troll-loaf and Egg-Trolls
- Secretly holds the power in Bergen Town

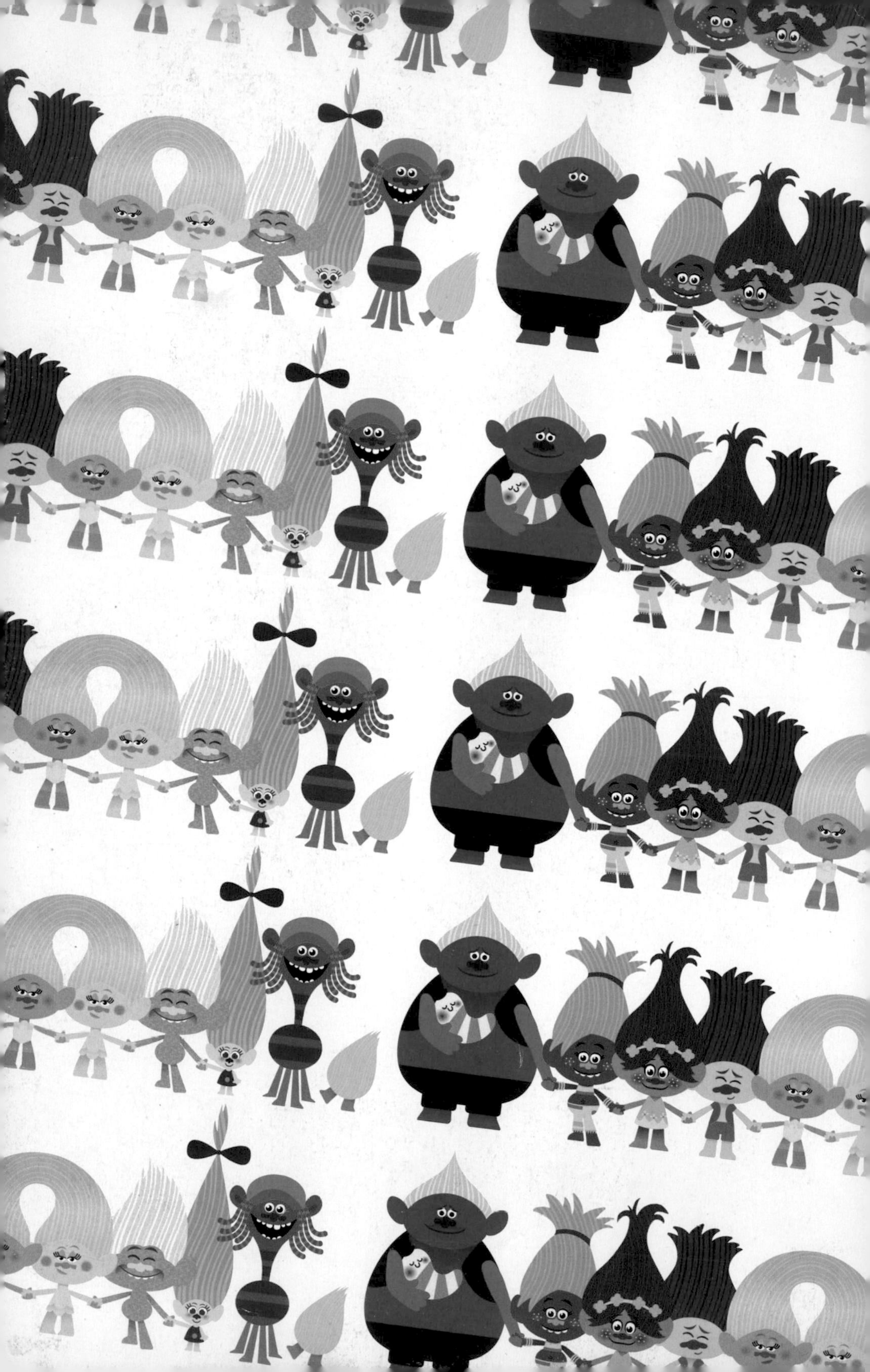

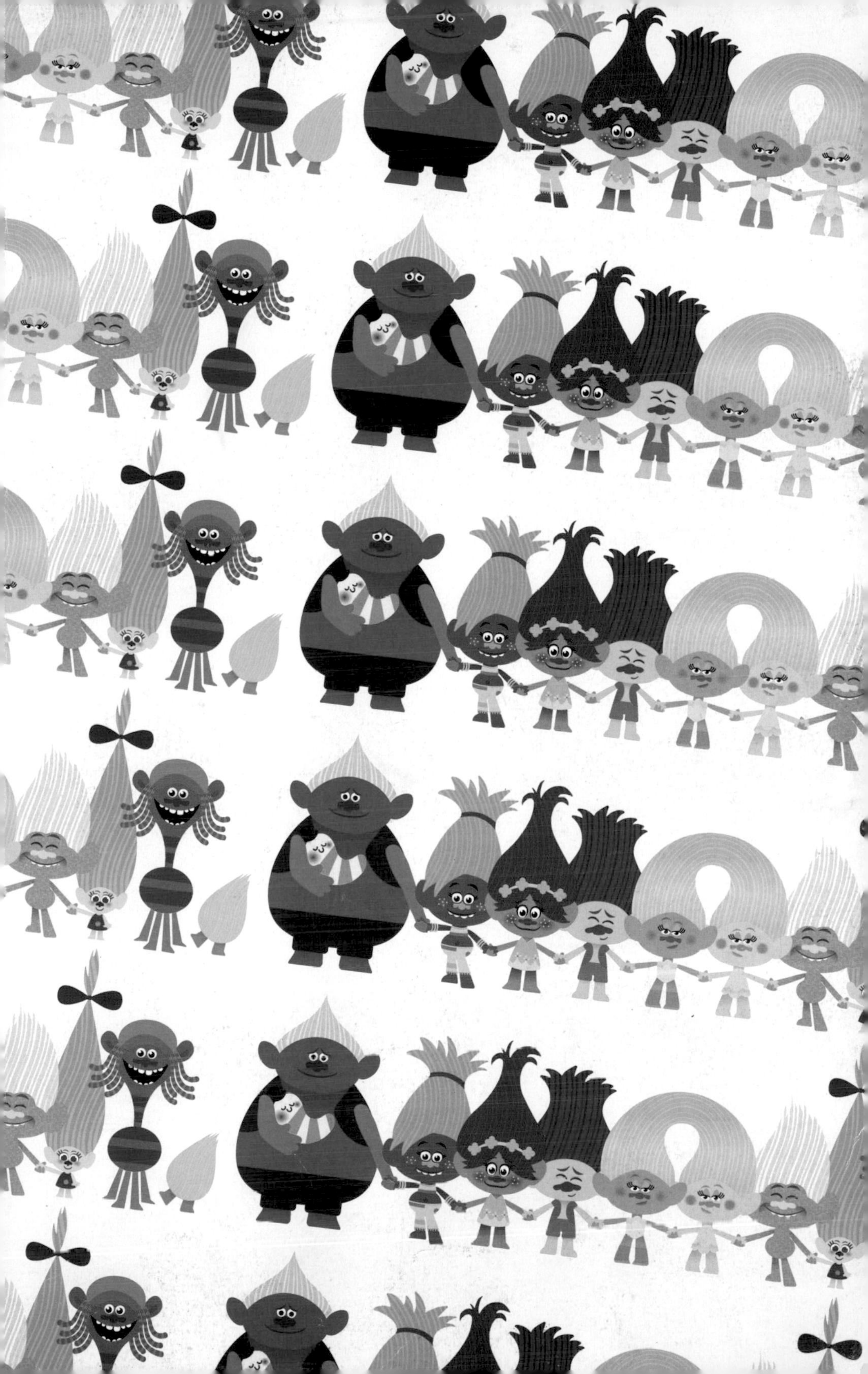

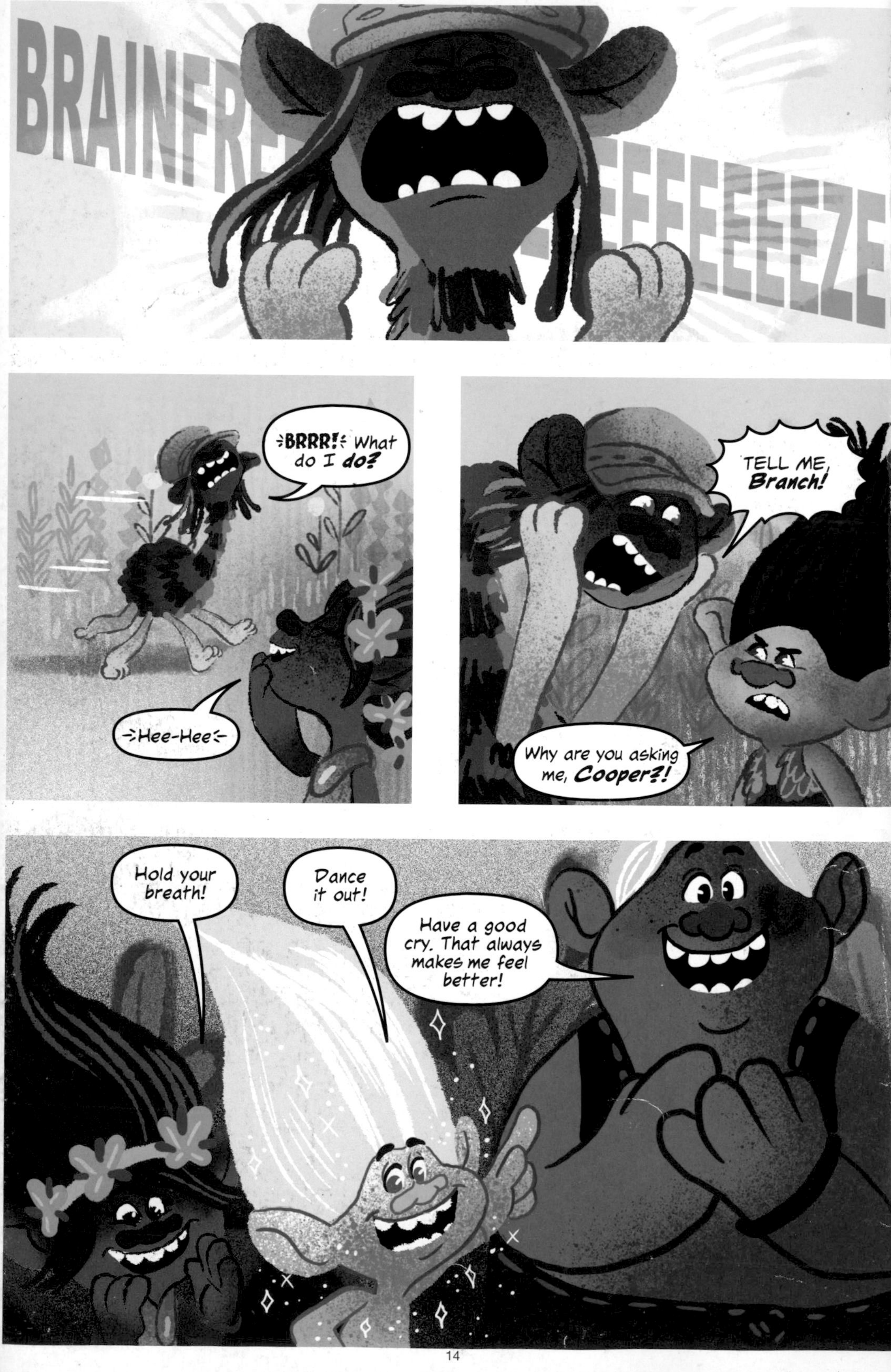
BRAINFRE EEEEEEEZE
BRRR! What do I do?
Hee-Hee
TELL ME, Branch!
Why are you asking me, Cooper?!
Hold your breath!
Dance it out!
Have a good cry. That always makes me feel better!

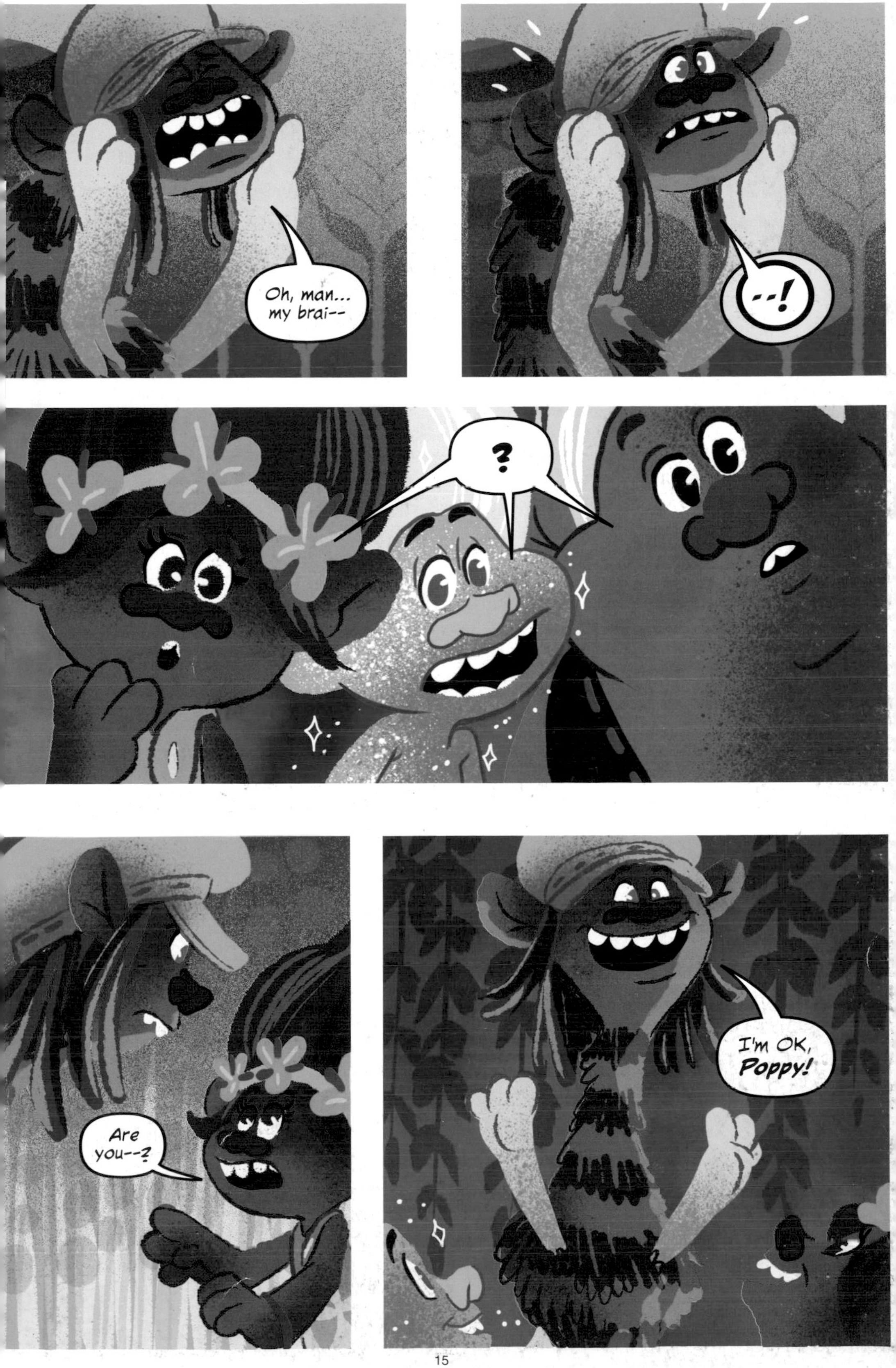
Oh, man...
my brai--
--!
?
Are
you--?
I'm OK,
Poppy!

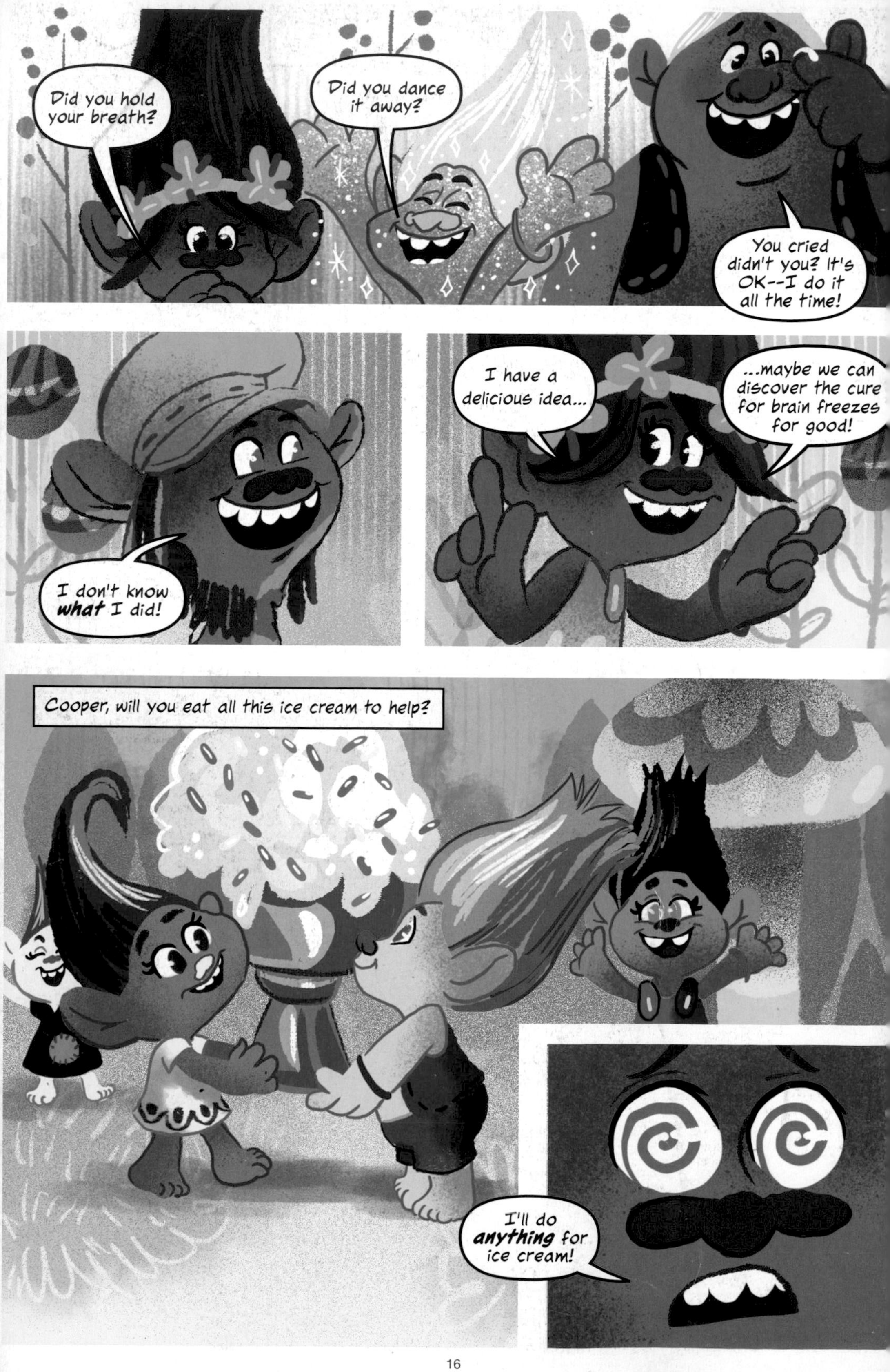

Did you hold your breath?
Did you dance it away?
You cried didn't you? It's OK--I do it all the time!
I don't know **what** I did!
I have a delicious idea...
...maybe we can discover the cure for brain freezes for good!
Cooper, will you eat all this ice cream to help?
I'll do **anything** for ice cream!

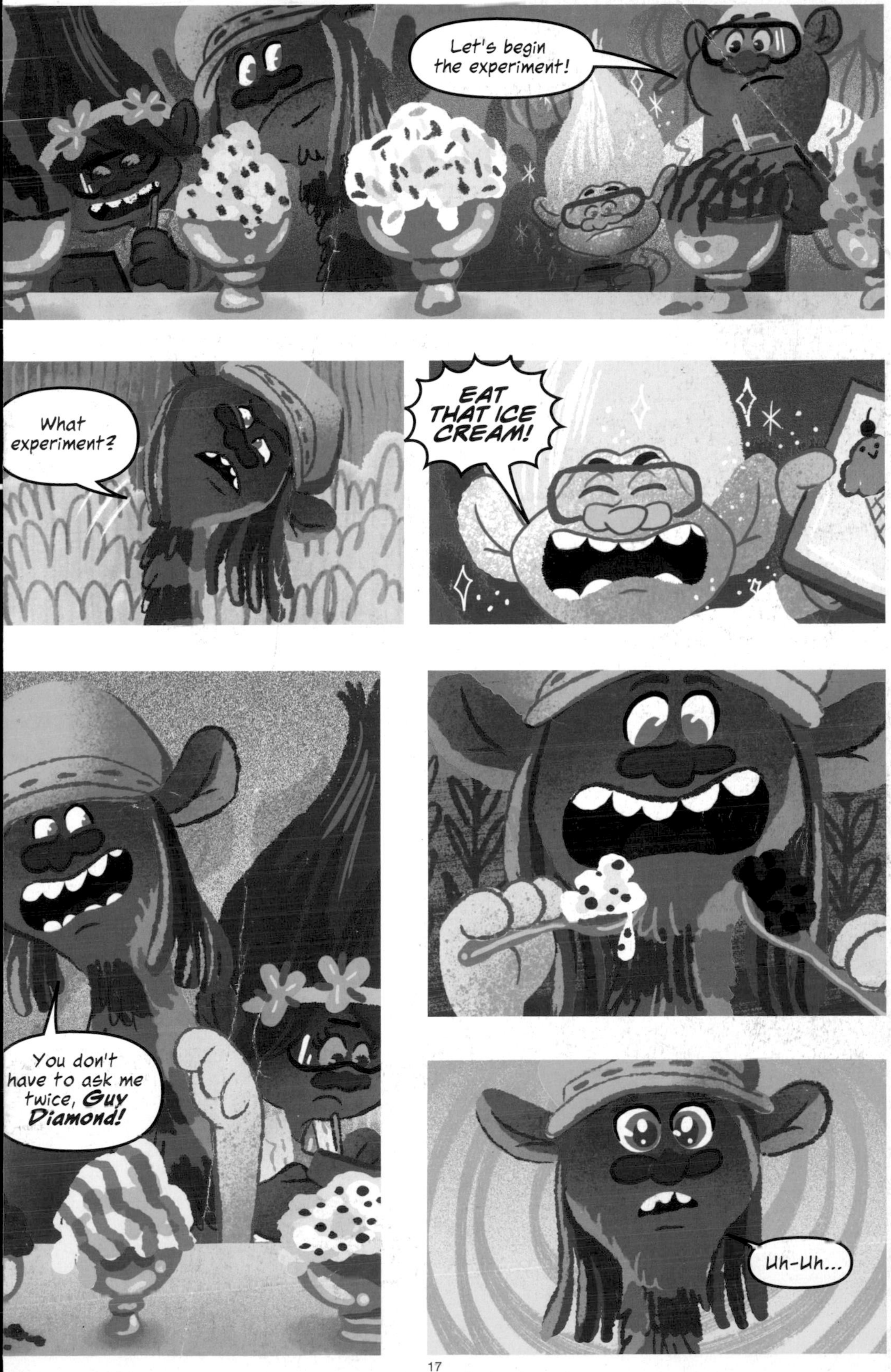
Let's begin the experiment!
What experiment?
EAT THAT ICE CREAM!
You don't have to ask me twice, Guy Diamond!
Uh-Uh...

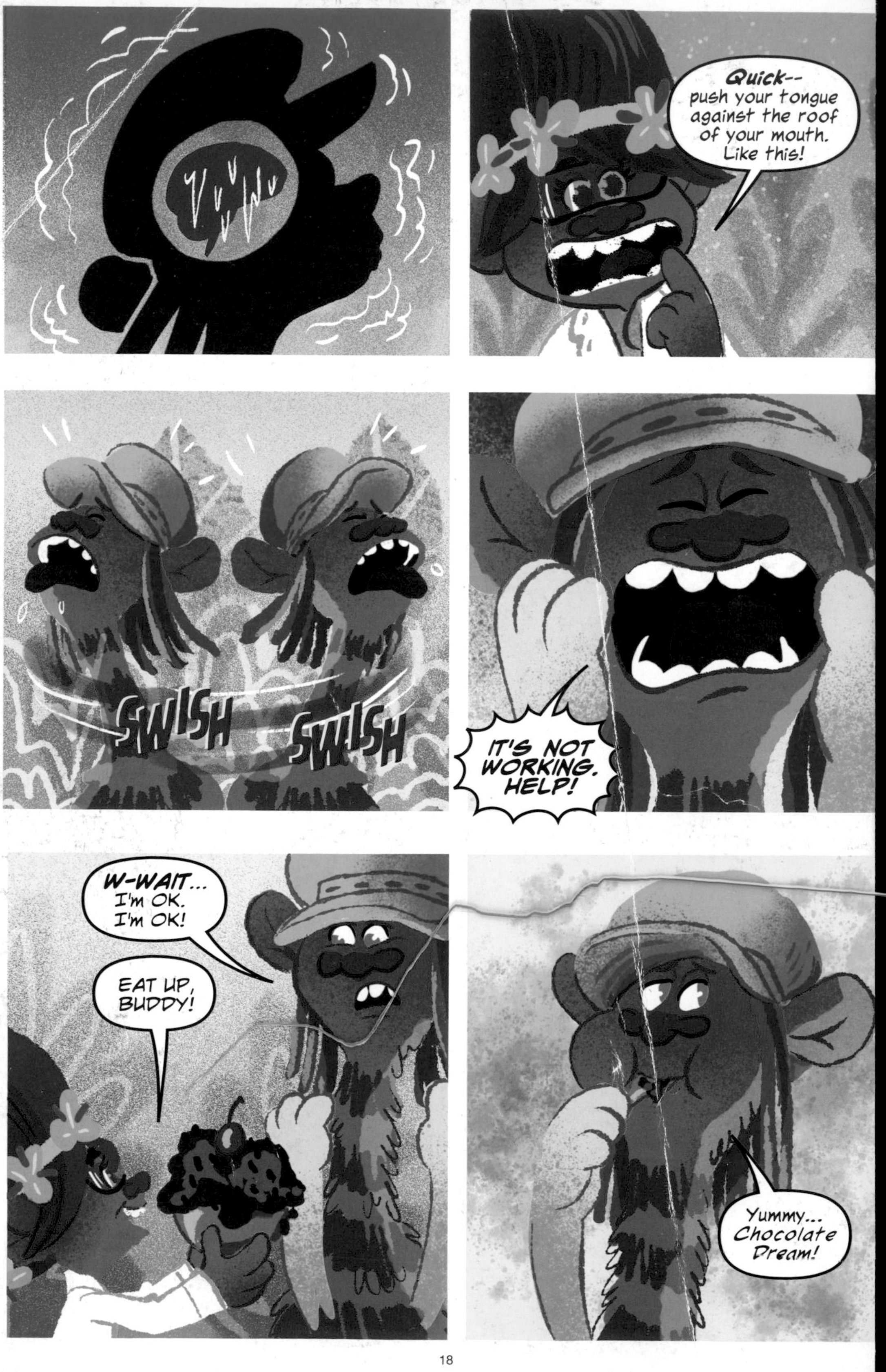

Quick--
push your tongue against the roof of your mouth. Like this!
SWISH
SWISH
IT'S NOT WORKING. HELP!
W-WAIT... I'm OK. I'm OK!
EAT UP, BUDDY!
Yummy... Chocolate Dream!

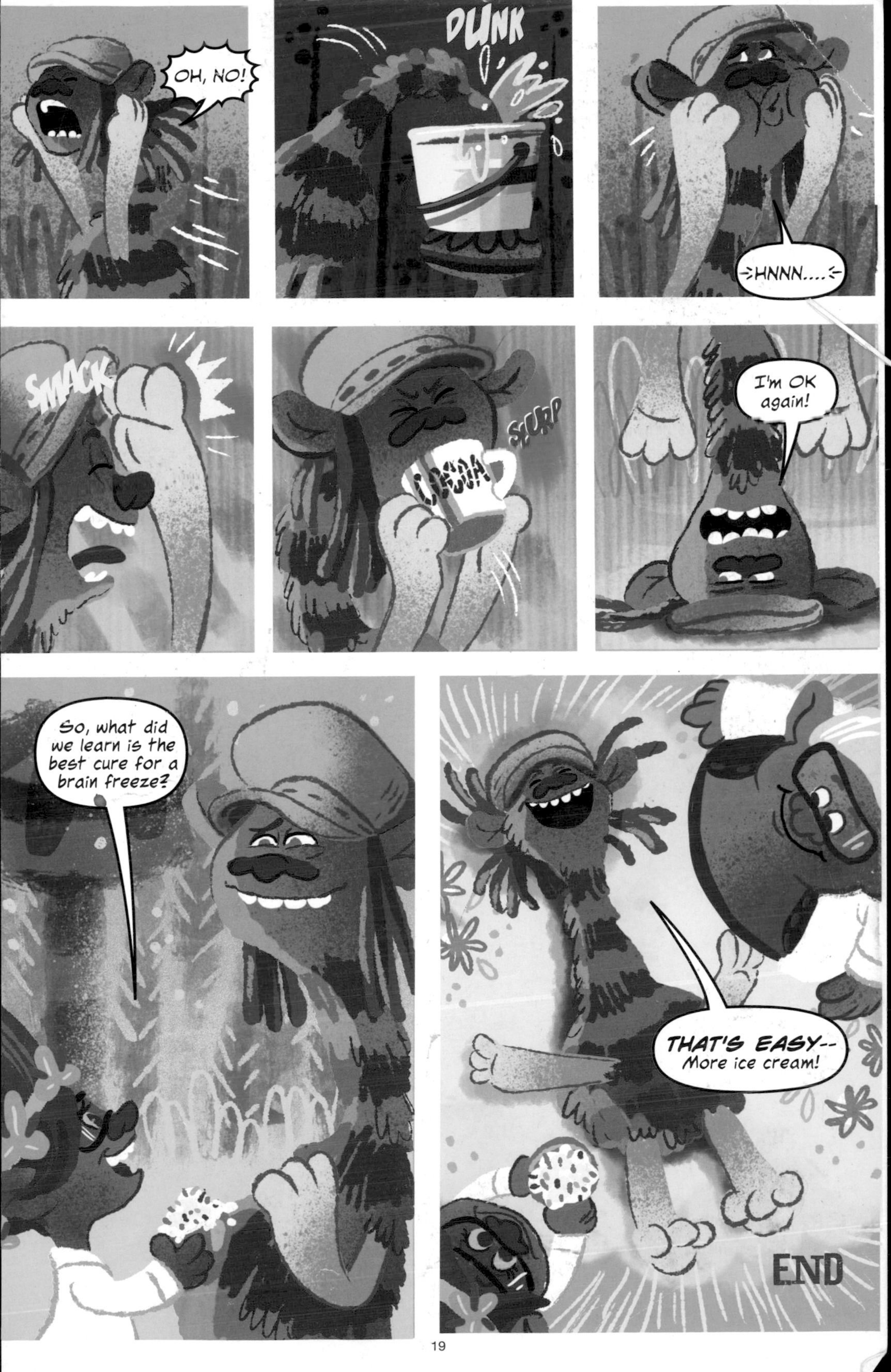
OH, NO!
DUNK
HNNN....
SMACK
SLURP
COCOA
I'm OK again!
So, what did we learn is the best cure for a brain freeze?
THAT'S EASY-- More ice cream!
END

WATCH OUT FOR HUGS

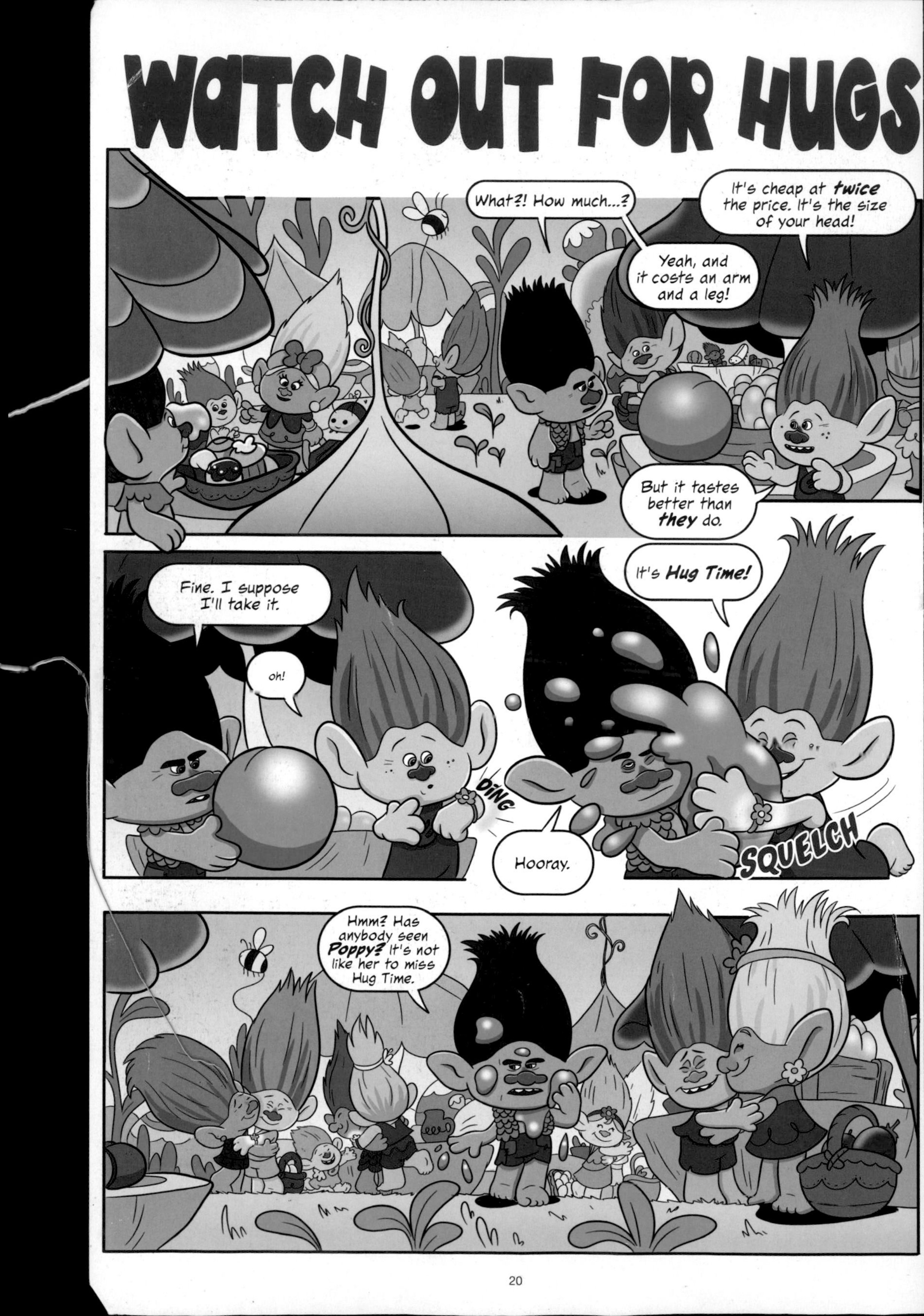

What?! How much...?
It's cheap at *twice* the price. It's the size of your head!
Yeah, and it costs an arm and a leg!
But it tastes better than *they* do.
Fine. I suppose I'll take it.
oh!
DING
It's *Hug Time!*
Hooray.
SQUELCH
Hmm? Has anybody seen *Poppy?* It's not like her to miss Hug Time.

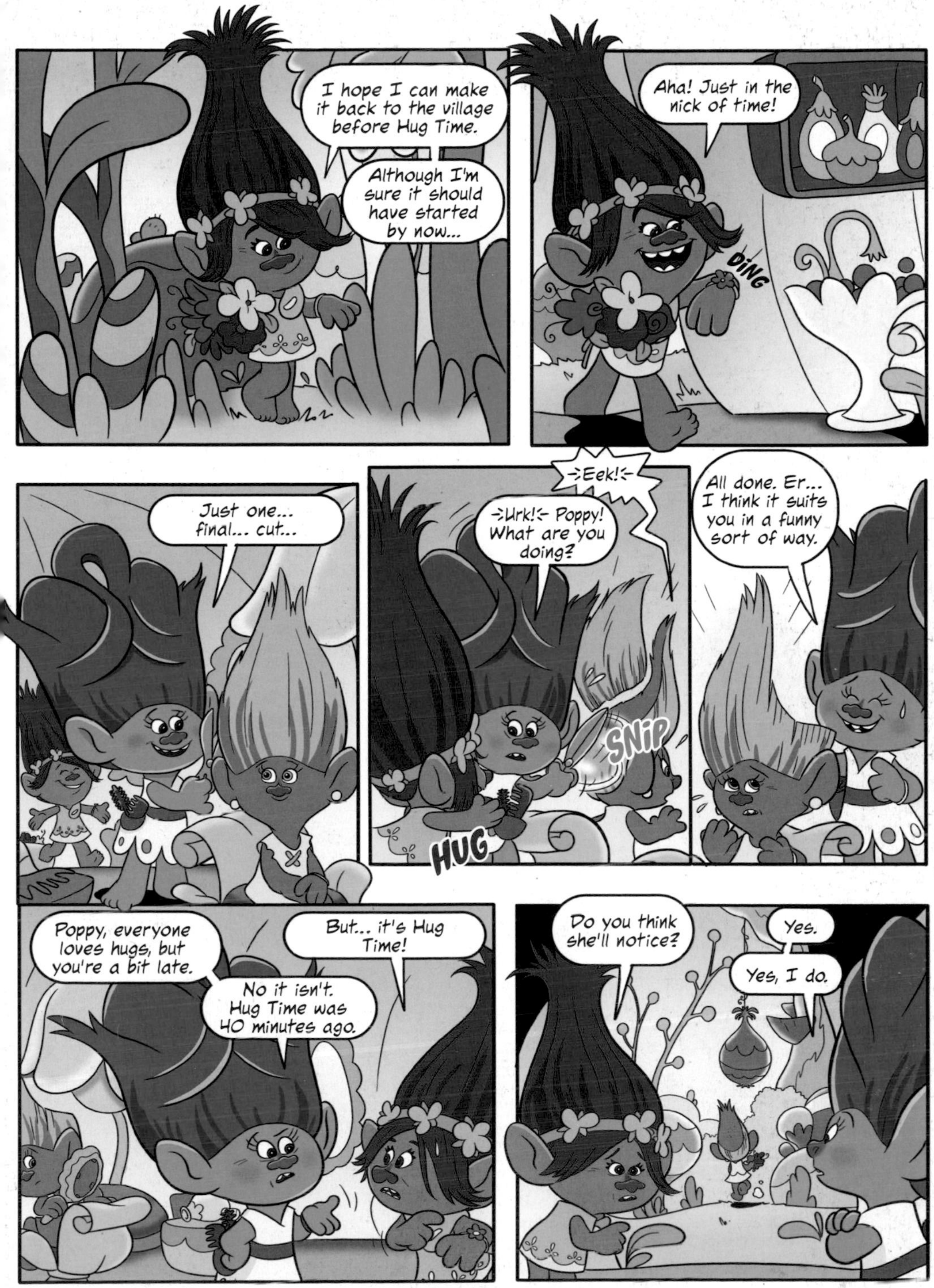
I hope I can make it back to the village before Hug Time.
Although I'm sure it should have started by now...
Aha! Just in the nick of time!
DING
Just one... final... cut...
-Eek!-
-Urk!- Poppy! What are you doing?
SNIP
HUG
All done. Er... I think it suits you in a funny sort of way.
Poppy, everyone loves hugs, but you're a bit late.
But... it's Hug Time!
No it isn't. Hug Time was 40 minutes ago.
Do you think she'll notice?
Yes.
Yes, I do.

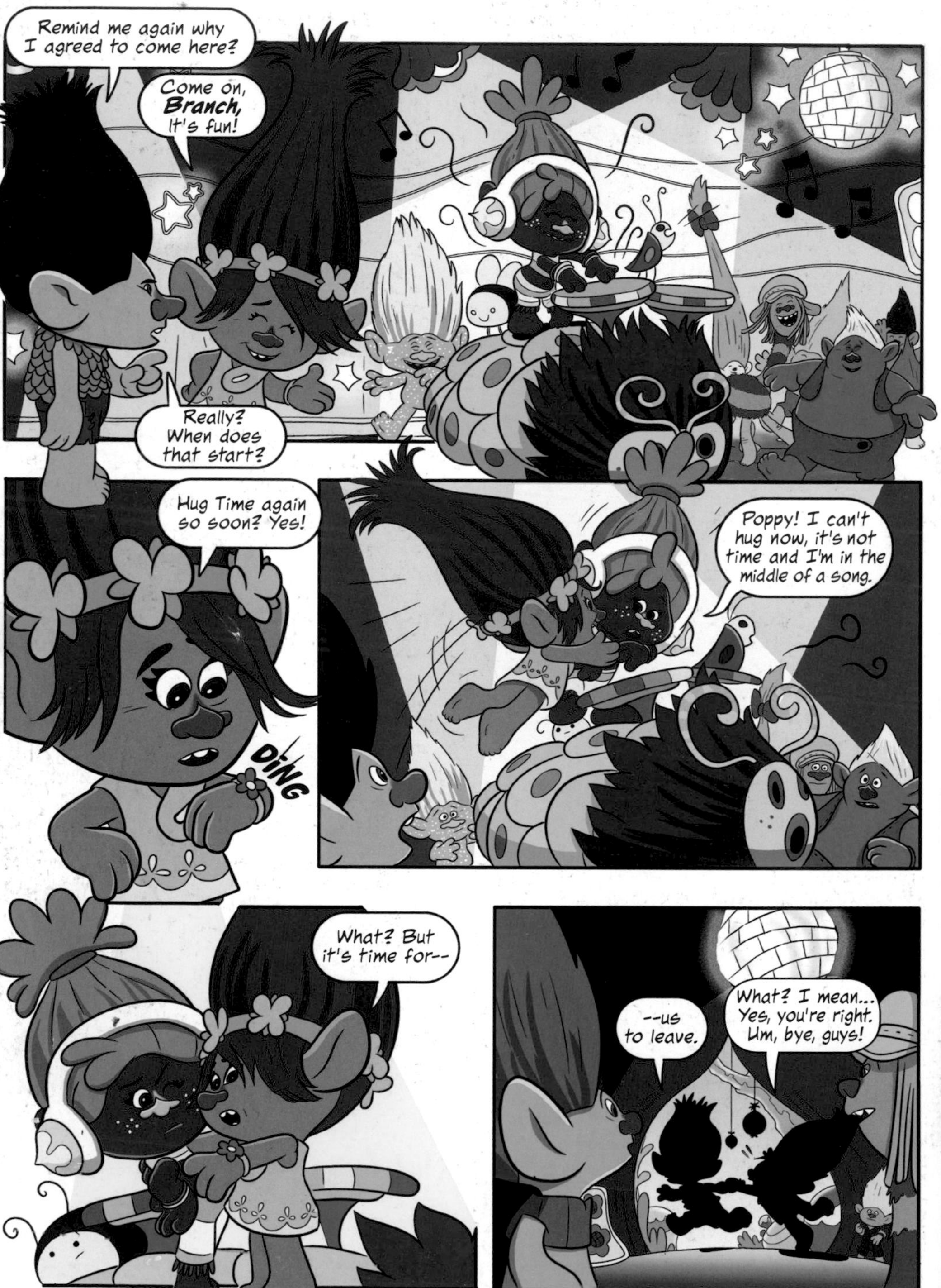
Remind me again why I agreed to come here?
Come on, **Branch,** it's fun!
Really? When does that start?
Hug Time again so soon? Yes!
DING
Poppy! I can't hug now, it's not time and I'm in the middle of a song.
What? But it's time for--
--us to leave.
What? I mean... Yes, you're right. Um, bye, guys!

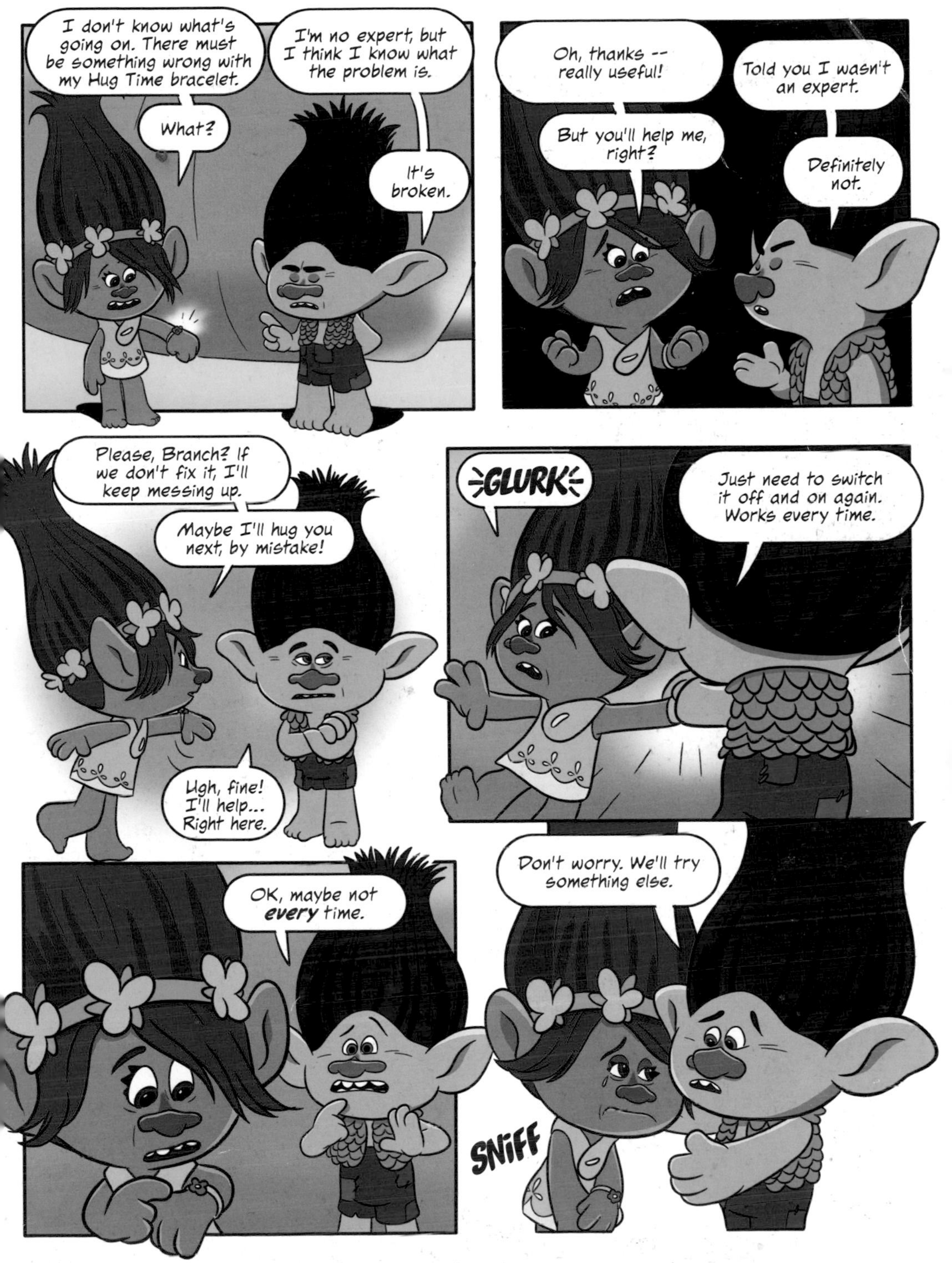

I don't know what's going on. There must be something wrong with my Hug Time bracelet.
I'm no expert, but I think I know what the problem is.
What?
It's broken.
Oh, thanks -- really useful!
Told you I wasn't an expert.
But you'll help me, right?
Definitely not.
Please, Branch? If we don't fix it, I'll keep messing up.
Maybe I'll hug you next, by mistake!
Ugh, fine! I'll help... Right here.
GLURK
Just need to switch it off and on again. Works every time.
OK, maybe not *every* time.
Don't worry. We'll try something else.
SNIFF

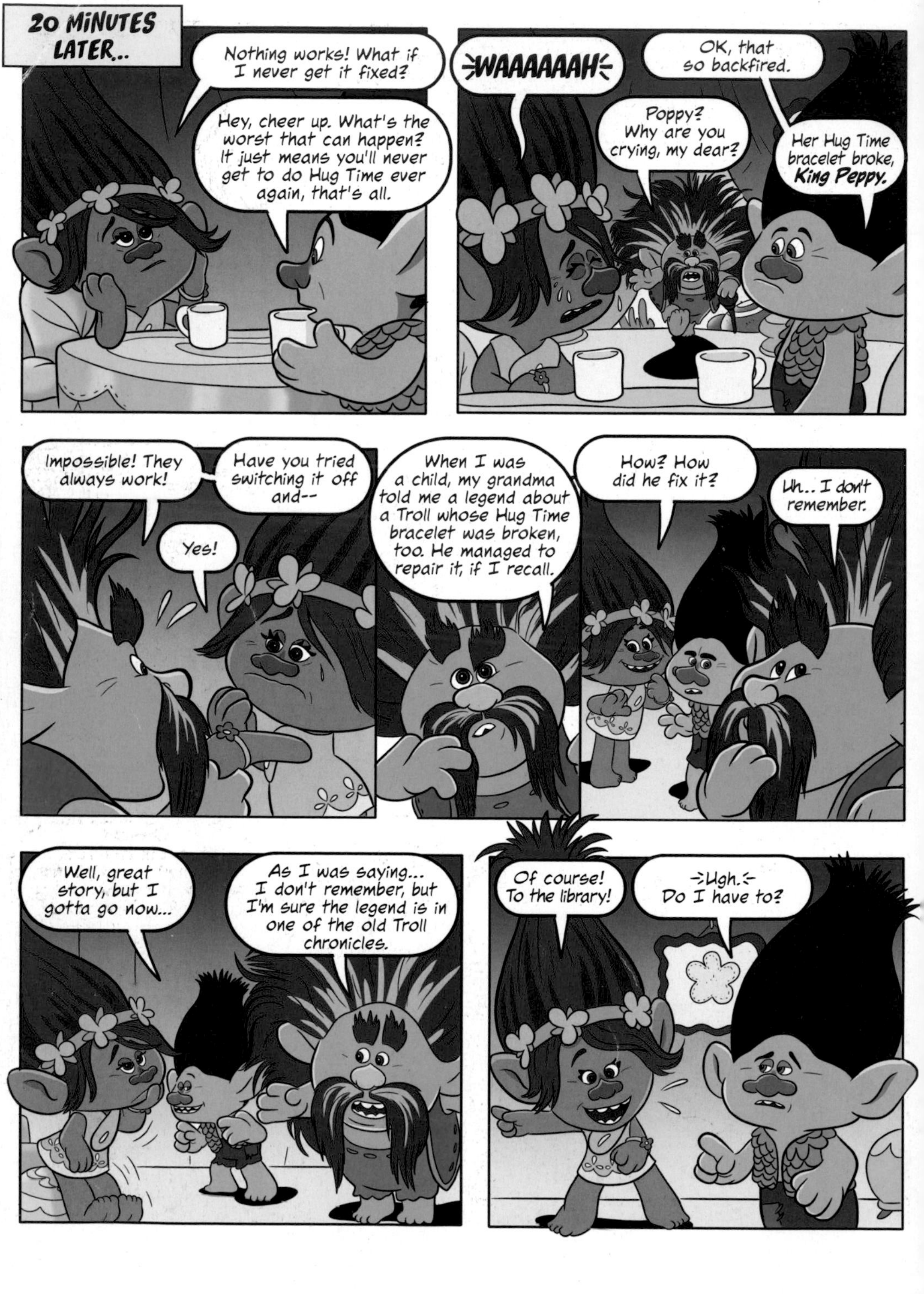
20 MINUTES LATER...
Nothing works! What if I never get it fixed?
Hey, cheer up. What's the worst that can happen? It just means you'll never get to do Hug Time ever again, that's all.
WAAAAAAH
OK, that so backfired.
Poppy? Why are you crying, my dear?
Her Hug Time bracelet broke, King Peppy.
Impossible! They always work!
Have you tried switching it off and--
Yes!
When I was a child, my grandma told me a legend about a Troll whose Hug Time bracelet was broken, too. He managed to repair it, if I recall.
How? How did he fix it?
Uh... I don't remember.
Well, great story, but I gotta go now...
As I was saying... I don't remember, but I'm sure the legend is in one of the old Troll chronicles.
Of course! To the library!
Ugh. Do I have to?

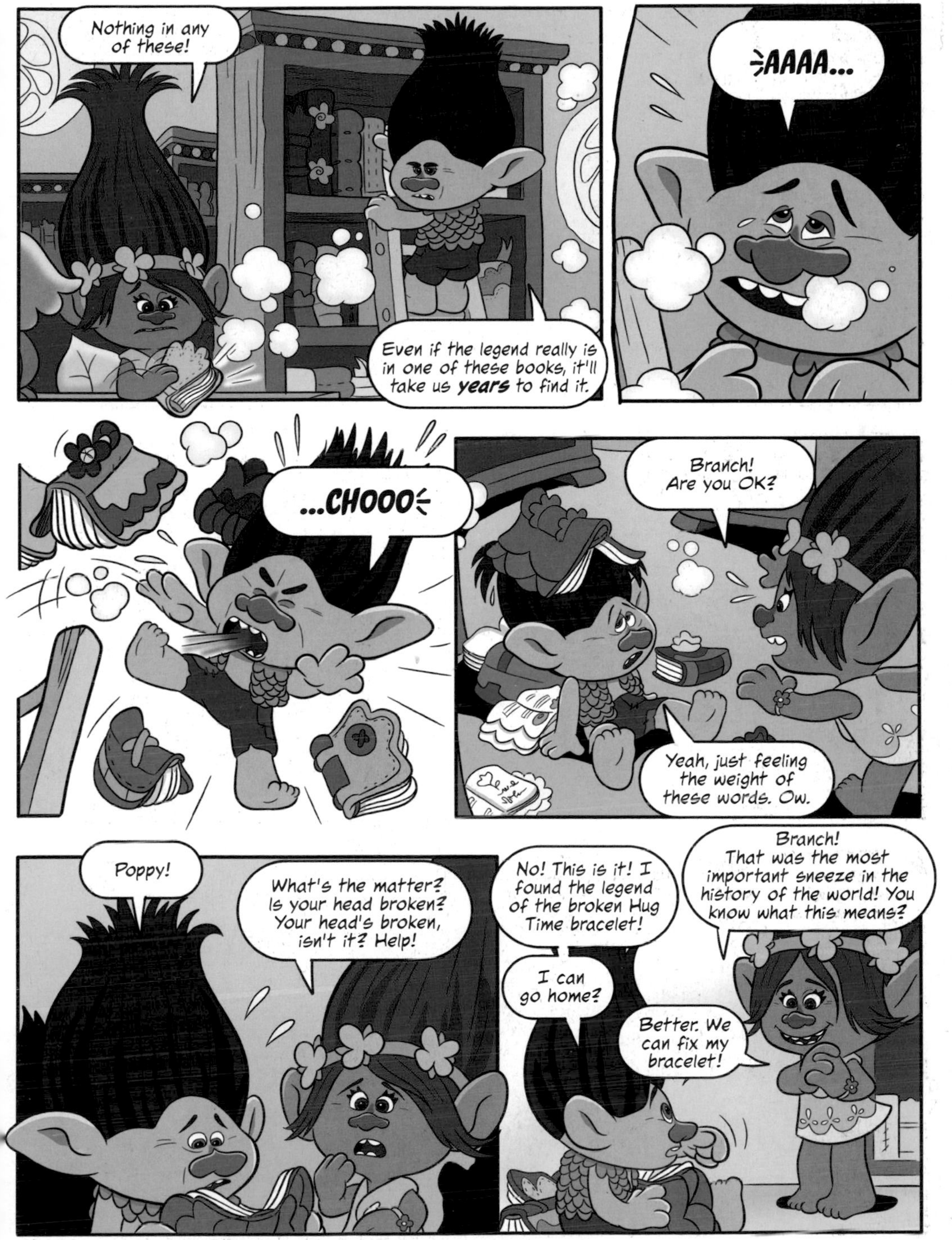
Nothing in any of these!
Even if the legend really is in one of these books, it'll take us *years* to find it.
AAAA...
...CHOOO
Branch! Are you OK?
Yeah, just feeling the weight of these words. Ow.
Poppy!
What's the matter? Is your head broken? Your head's broken, isn't it? Help!
No! This is it! I found the legend of the broken Hug Time bracelet!
I can go home?
Branch! That was the most important sneeze in the history of the world! You know what this means?
Better. We can fix my bracelet!

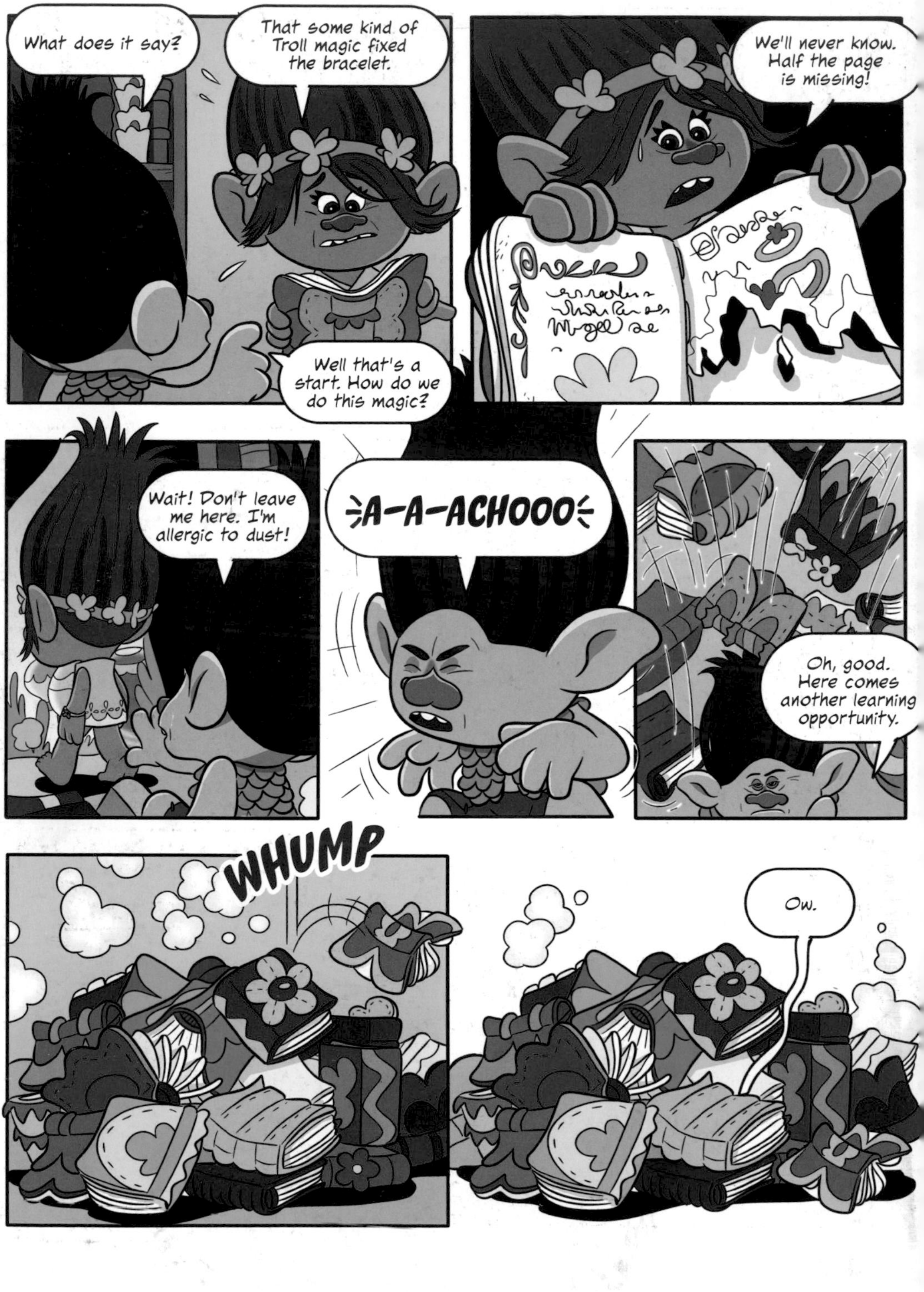

What does it say?
That some kind of Troll magic fixed the bracelet.
Well that's a start. How do we do this magic?
We'll never know. Half the page is missing!
Wait! Don't leave me here. I'm allergic to dust!
A-A-ACHOOO
Oh, good. Here comes another learning opportunity.
WHUMP
Ow.

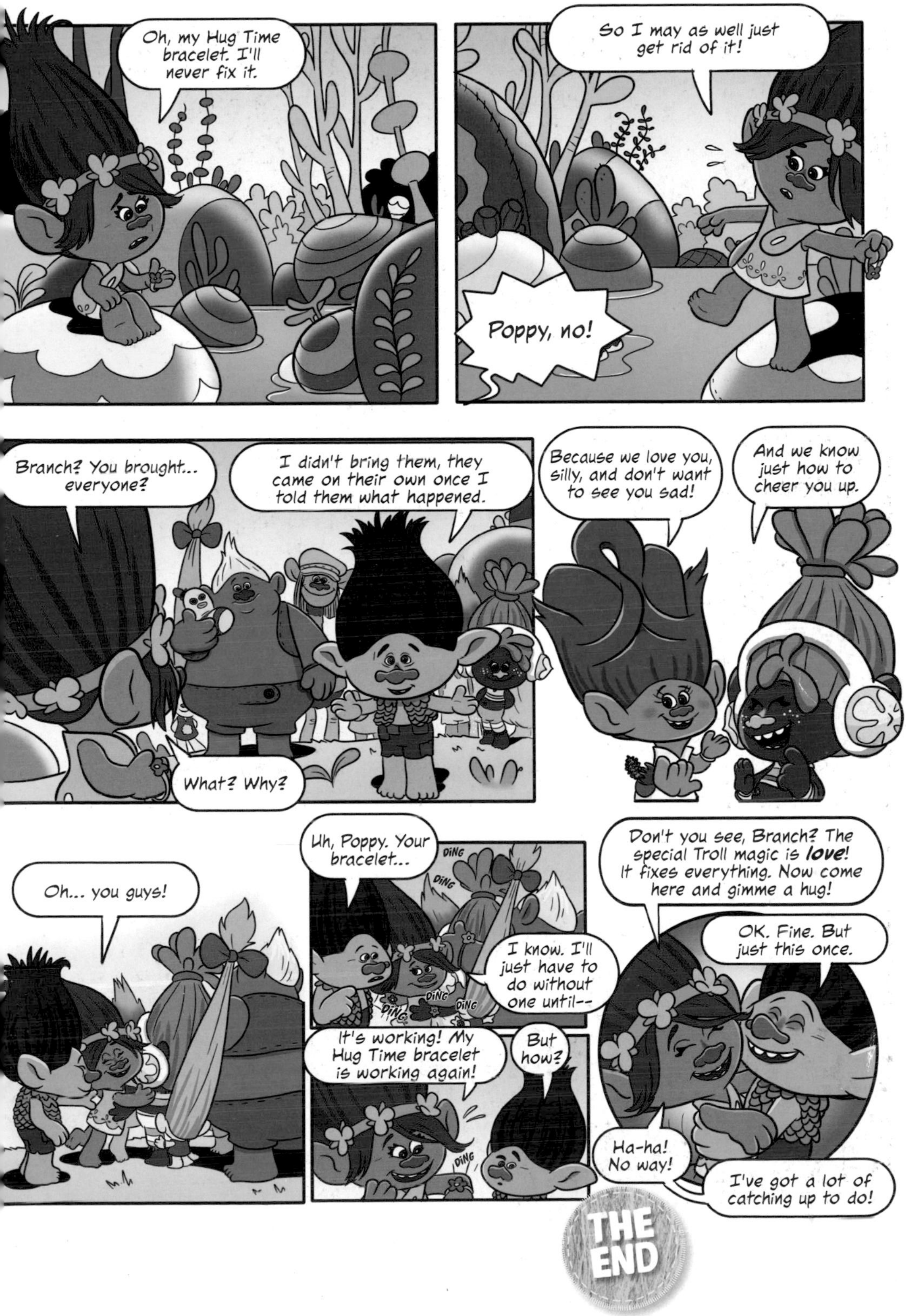

Oh, my Hug Time bracelet. I'll never fix it.
So I may as well just get rid of it!
Poppy, no!
Branch? You brought... everyone?
I didn't bring them, they came on their own once I told them what happened.
What? Why?
Because we love you, silly, and don't want to see you sad!
And we know just how to cheer you up.
Oh... you guys!
Uh, Poppy. Your bracelet...
DING
DING
I know. I'll just have to do without one until--
DING
DING
DING
It's working! My Hug Time bracelet is working again!
But how?
DING
Don't you see, Branch? The special Troll magic is **love**! It fixes everything. Now come here and gimme a hug!
OK. Fine. But just this once.
Ha-ha! No way!
I've got a lot of catching up to do!
THE END

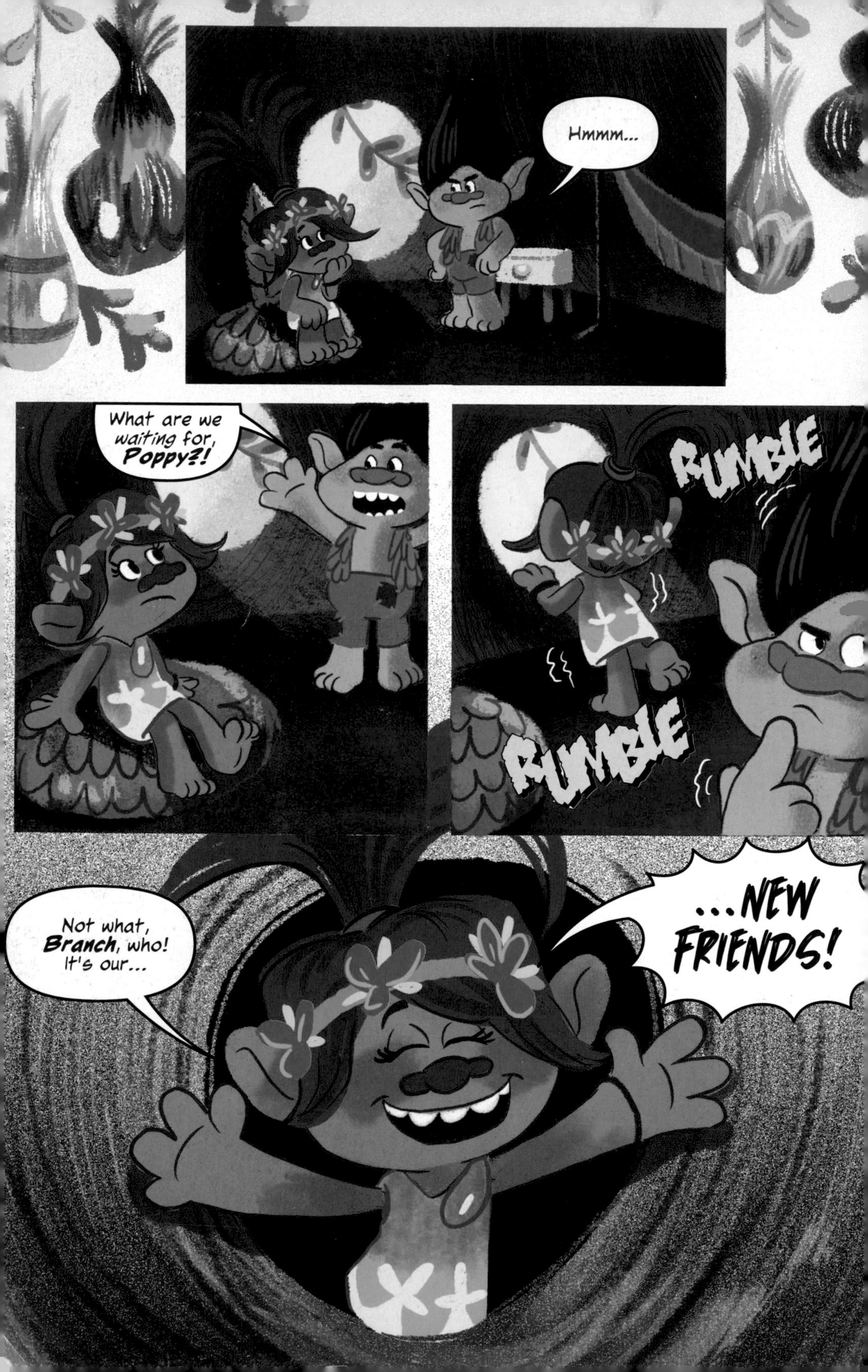
Hmmm...
What are we waiting for, Poppy?!
RUMBLE
RUMBLE
Not what, Branch, who! It's our...
...NEW FRIENDS!

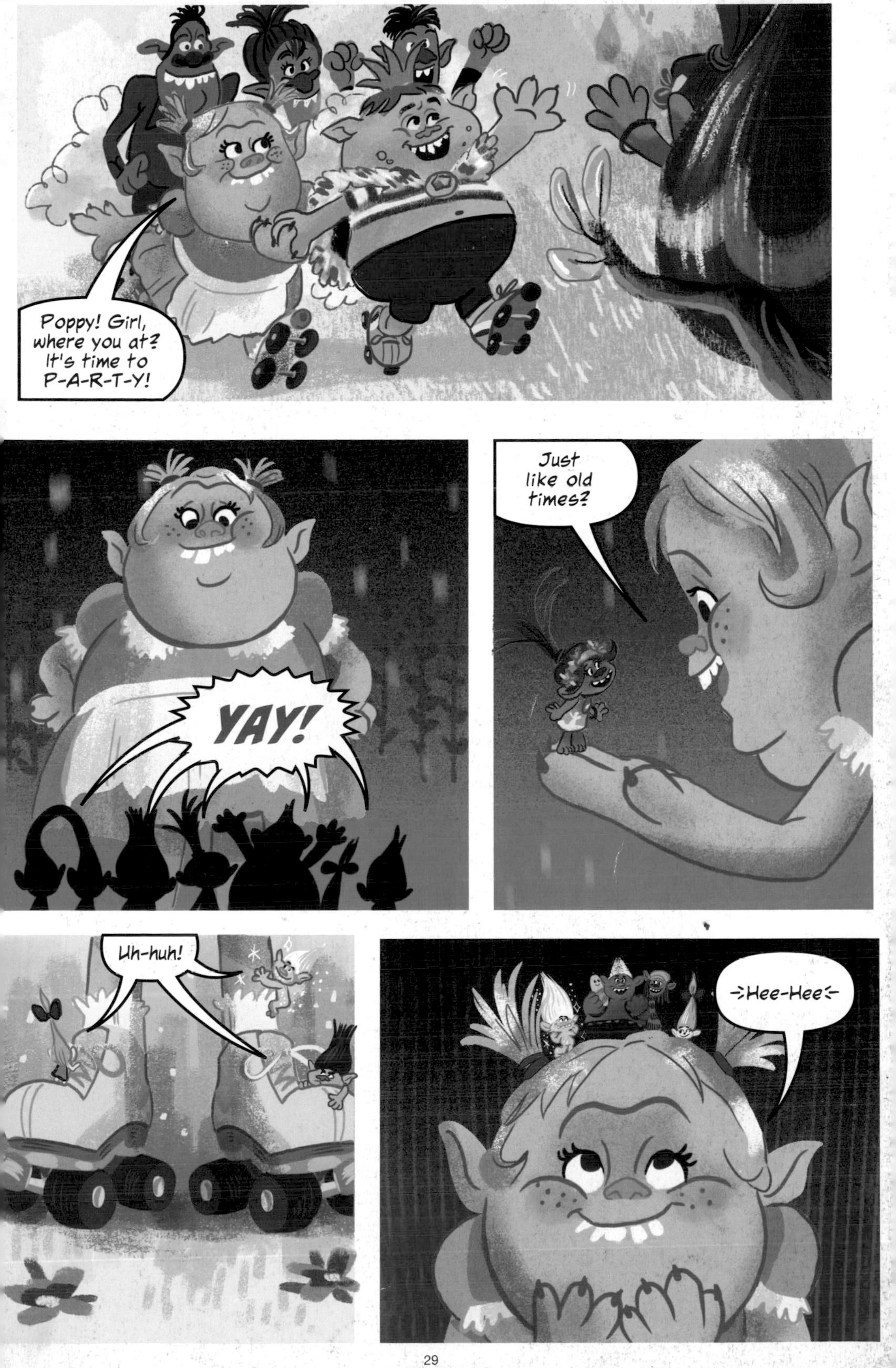
Poppy! Girl, where you at? It's time to P-A-R-T-Y!
YAY!
Just like old times?
Uh-huh!
Hee-Hee

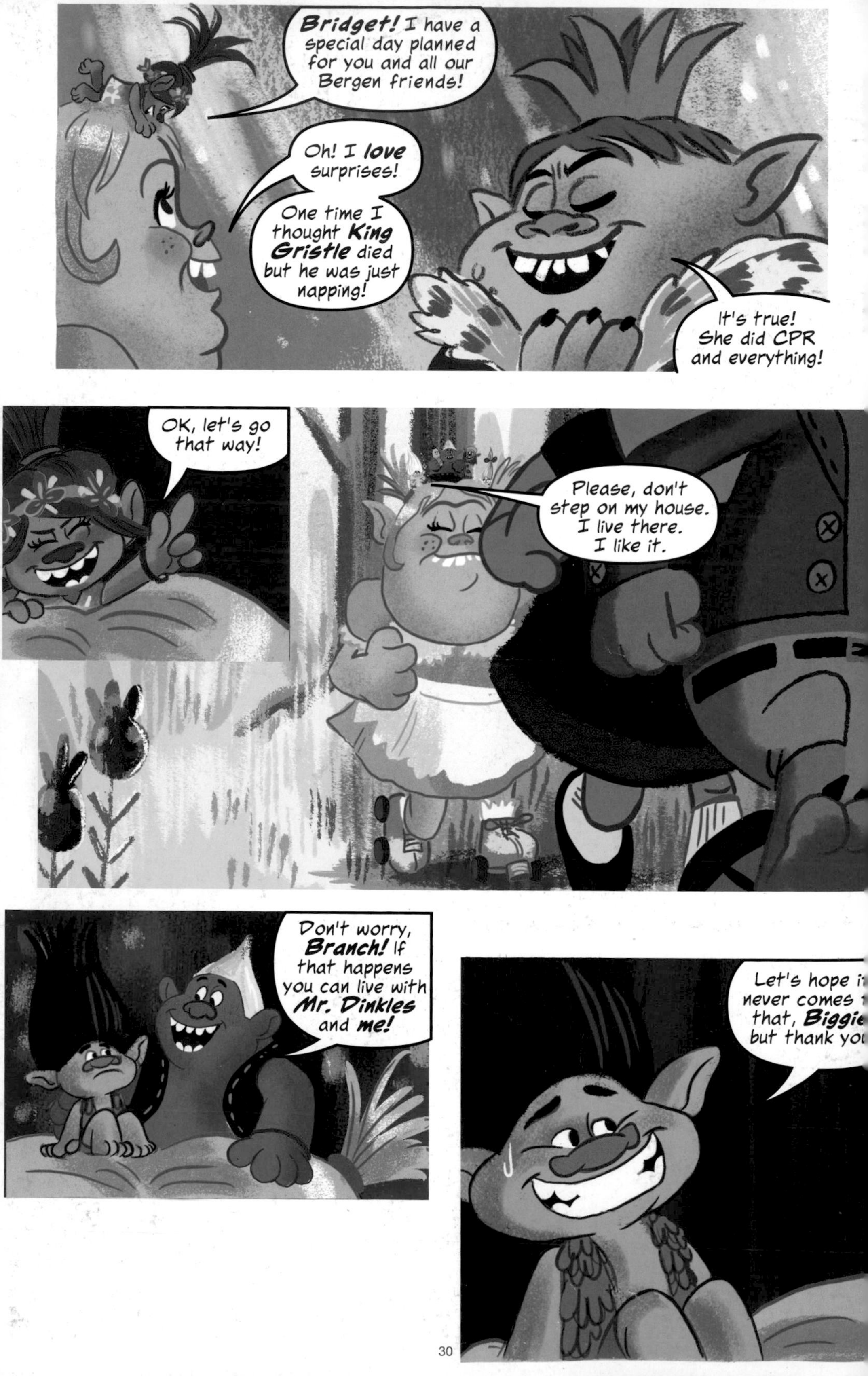

Bridget! I have a special day planned for you and all our Bergen friends!
Oh! I love surprises!
One time I thought King Gristle died but he was just napping!
It's true! She did CPR and everything!
OK, let's go that way!
Please, don't step on my house. I live there. I like it.
Don't worry, Branch! If that happens you can live with Mr. Dinkles and me!
Let's hope i never comes t that, Biggie but thank yo

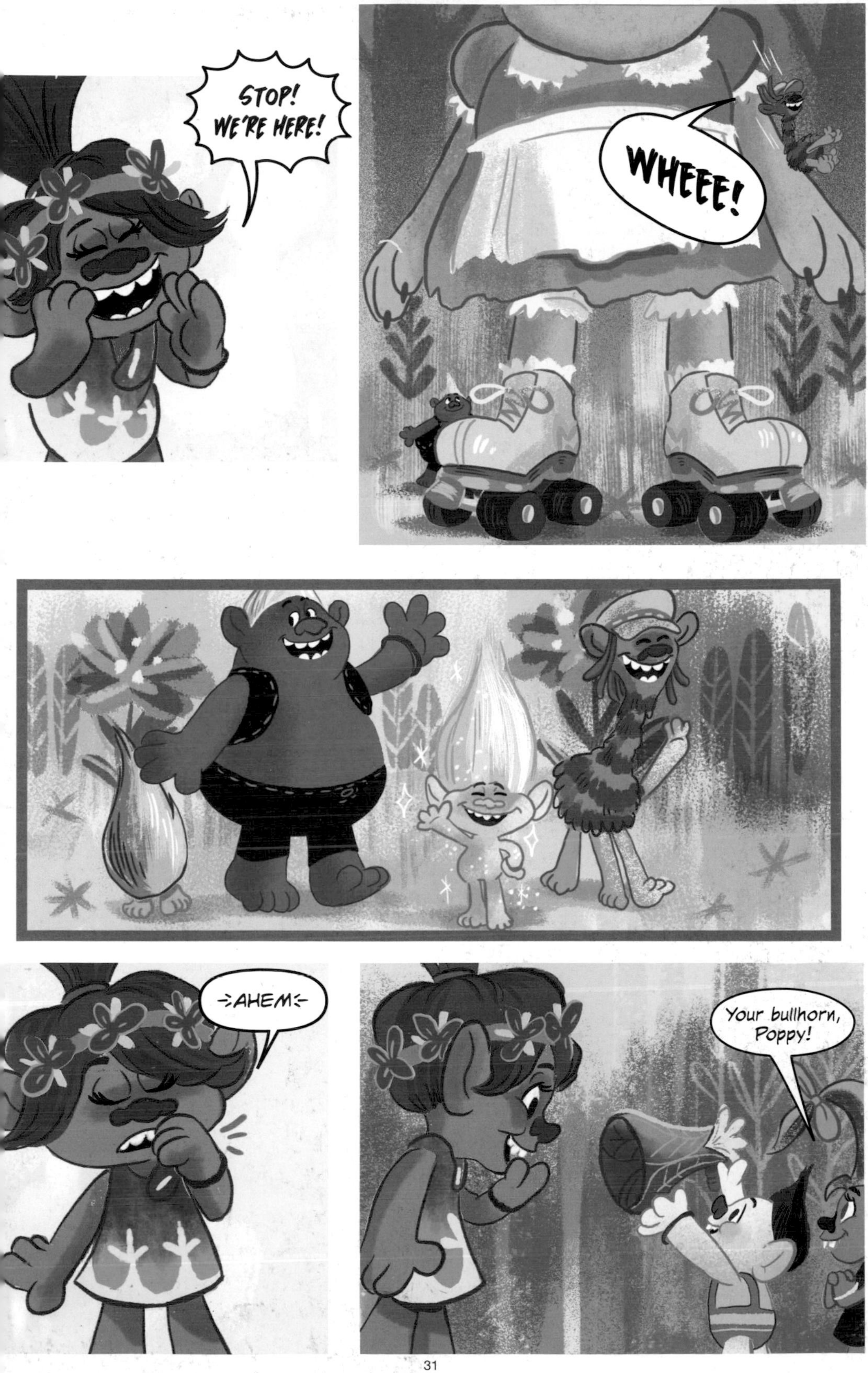
STOP! WE'RE HERE!
WHEEEE!
AHEM
Your bullhorn, Poppy!

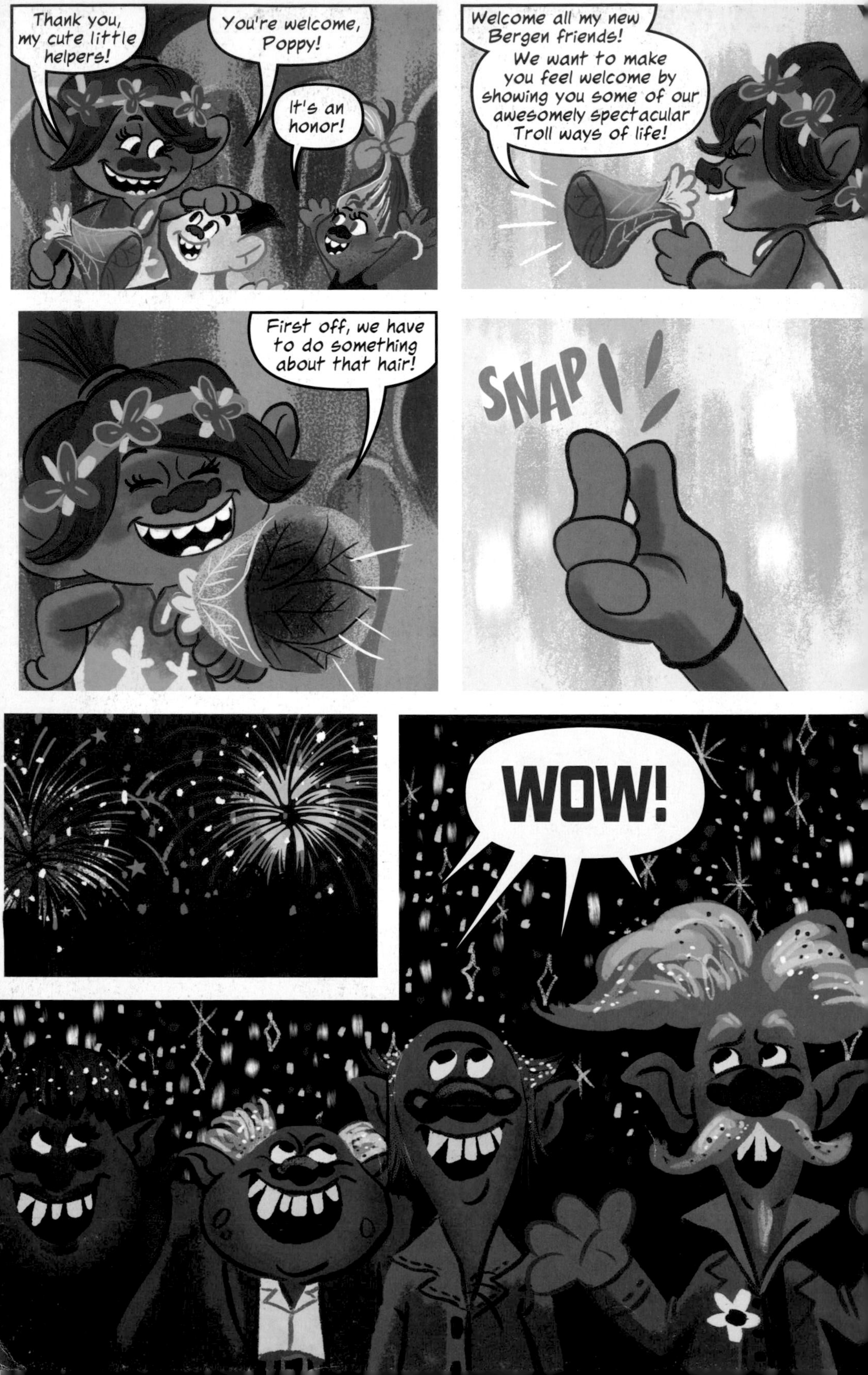
Thank you, my cute little helpers!
You're welcome, Poppy!
It's an honor!
Welcome all my new Bergen friends!
We want to make you feel welcome by showing you some of our awesomely spectacular Troll ways of life!
First off, we have to do something about that hair!
SNAP
WOW!

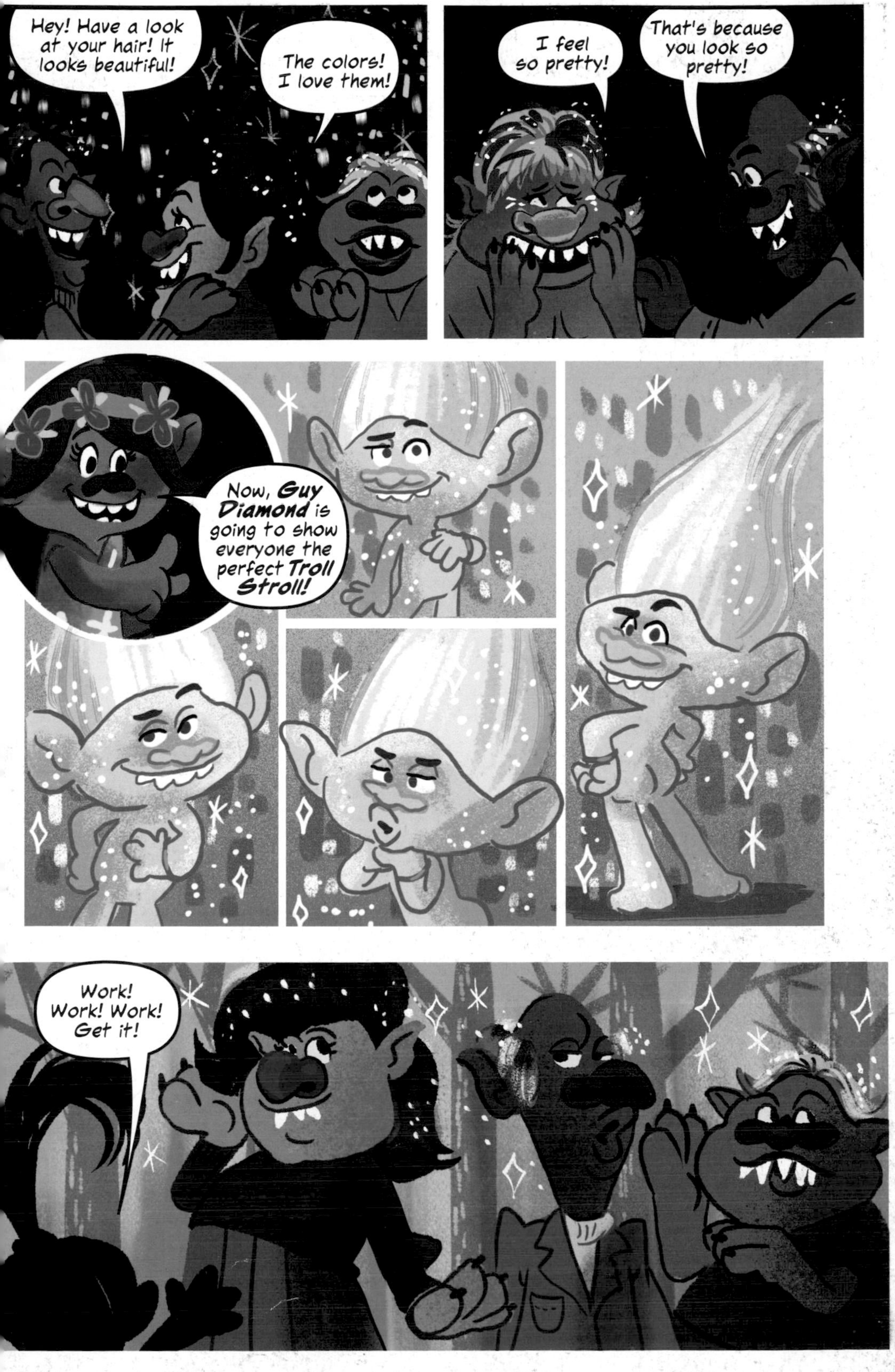
Hey! Have a look at your hair! It looks beautiful!
The colors! I love them!
I feel so pretty!
That's because you look so pretty!
Now, **Guy Diamond** is going to show everyone the perfect ***Troll Stroll!***
Work! Work! Work! Get it!

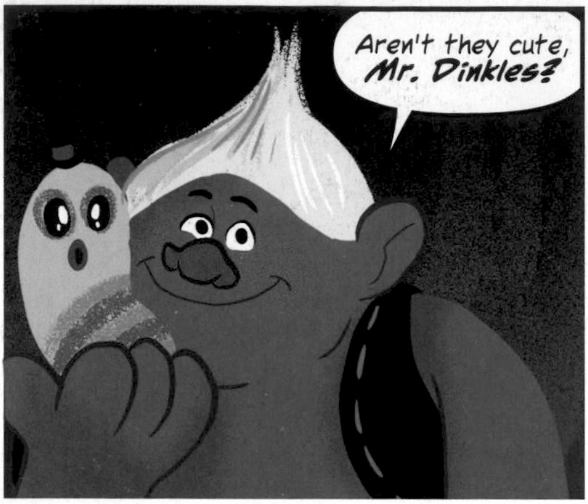
Aren't they cute, **Mr. Dinkles?**

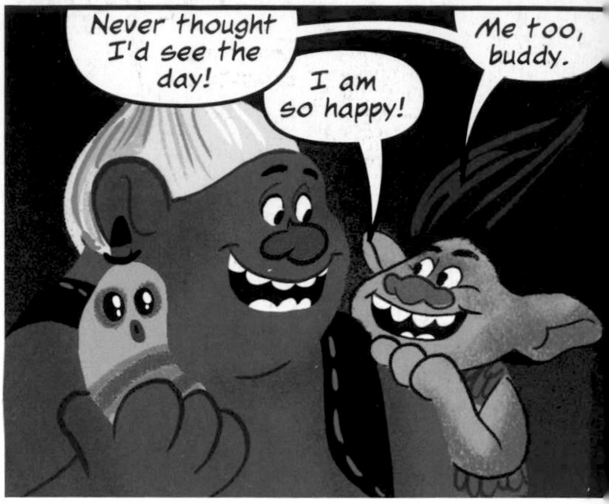
Never thought I'd see the day!
I am so happy!
Me too, buddy.

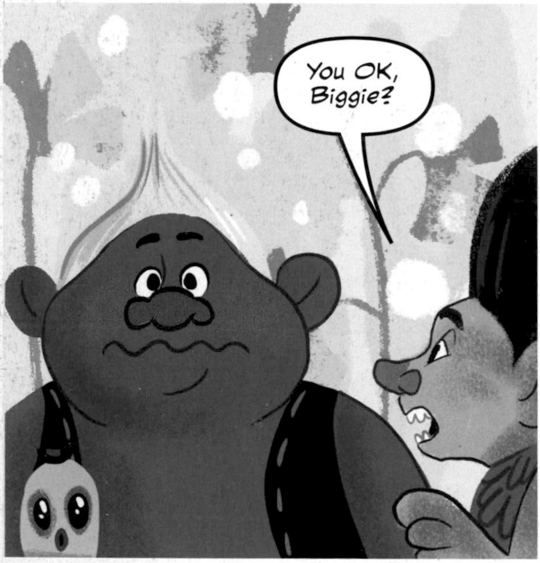
You OK, Biggie?

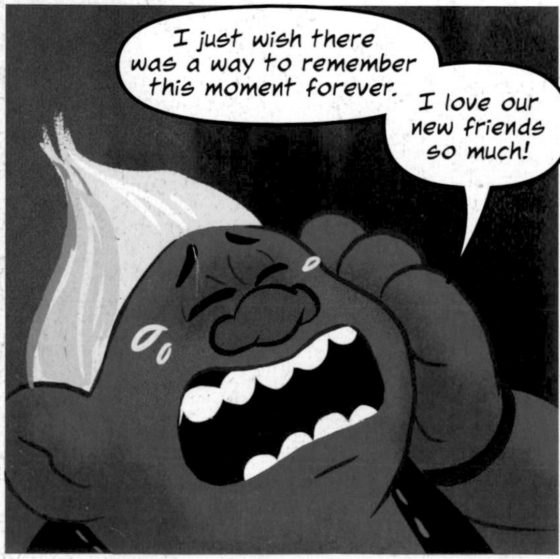
I just wish there was a way to remember this moment forever.
I love our new friends so much!

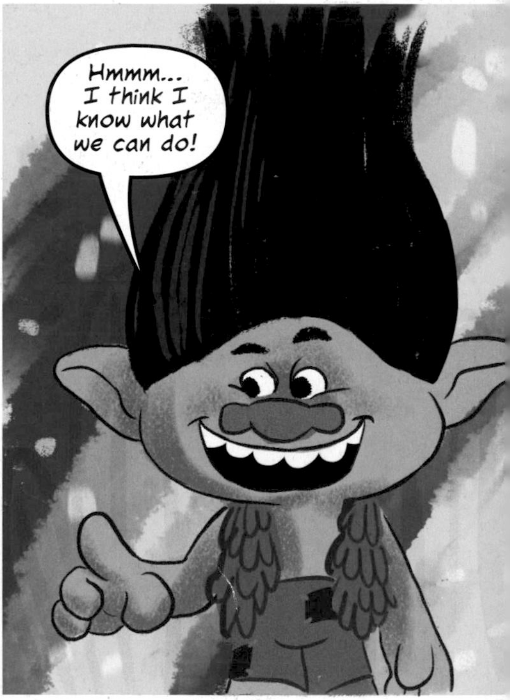
Hmmm... I think I know what we can do!

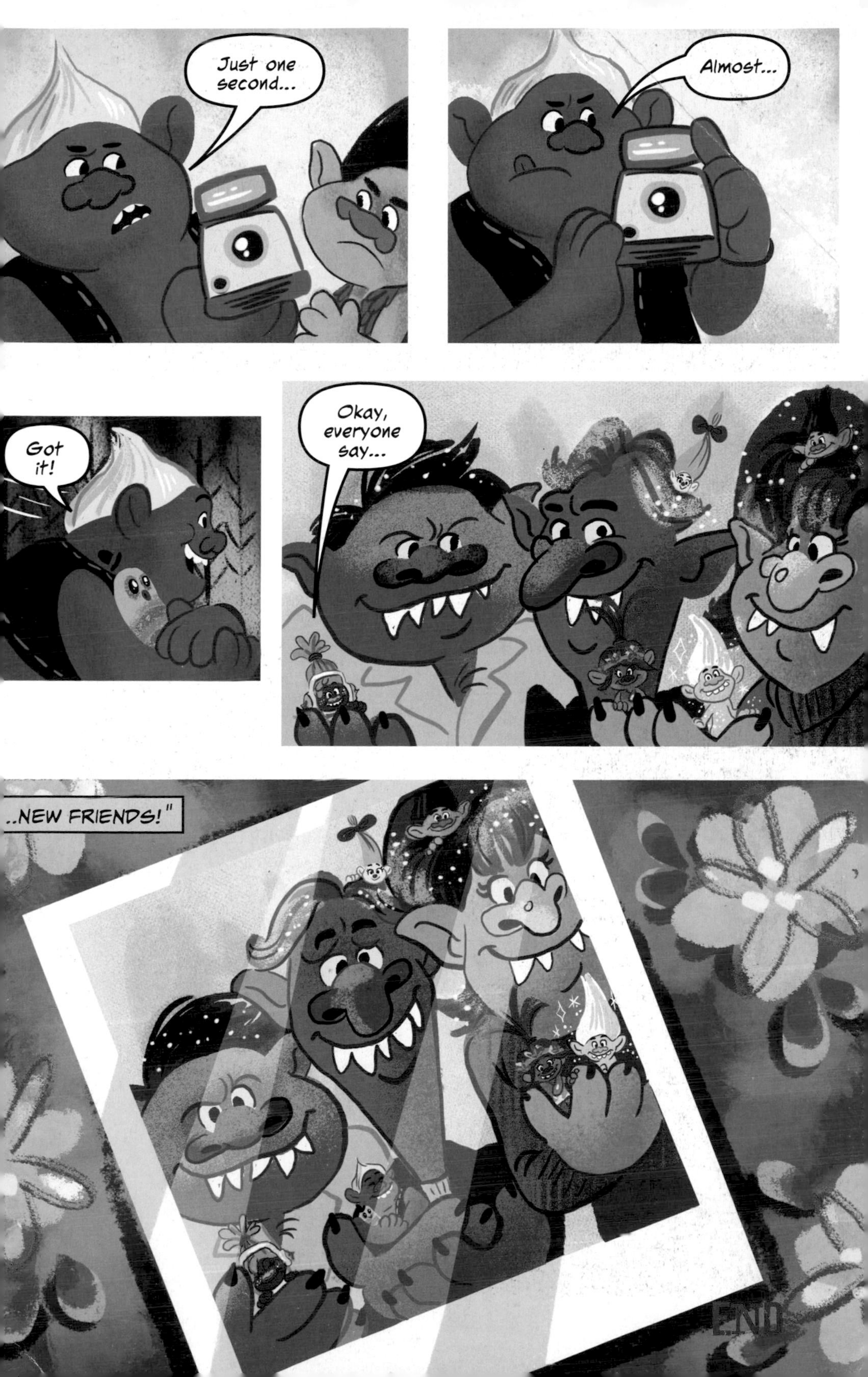
Just one second...
Almost...
Got it!
Okay, everyone say...
..NEW FRIENDS!"
END

MR. DINK-ILL

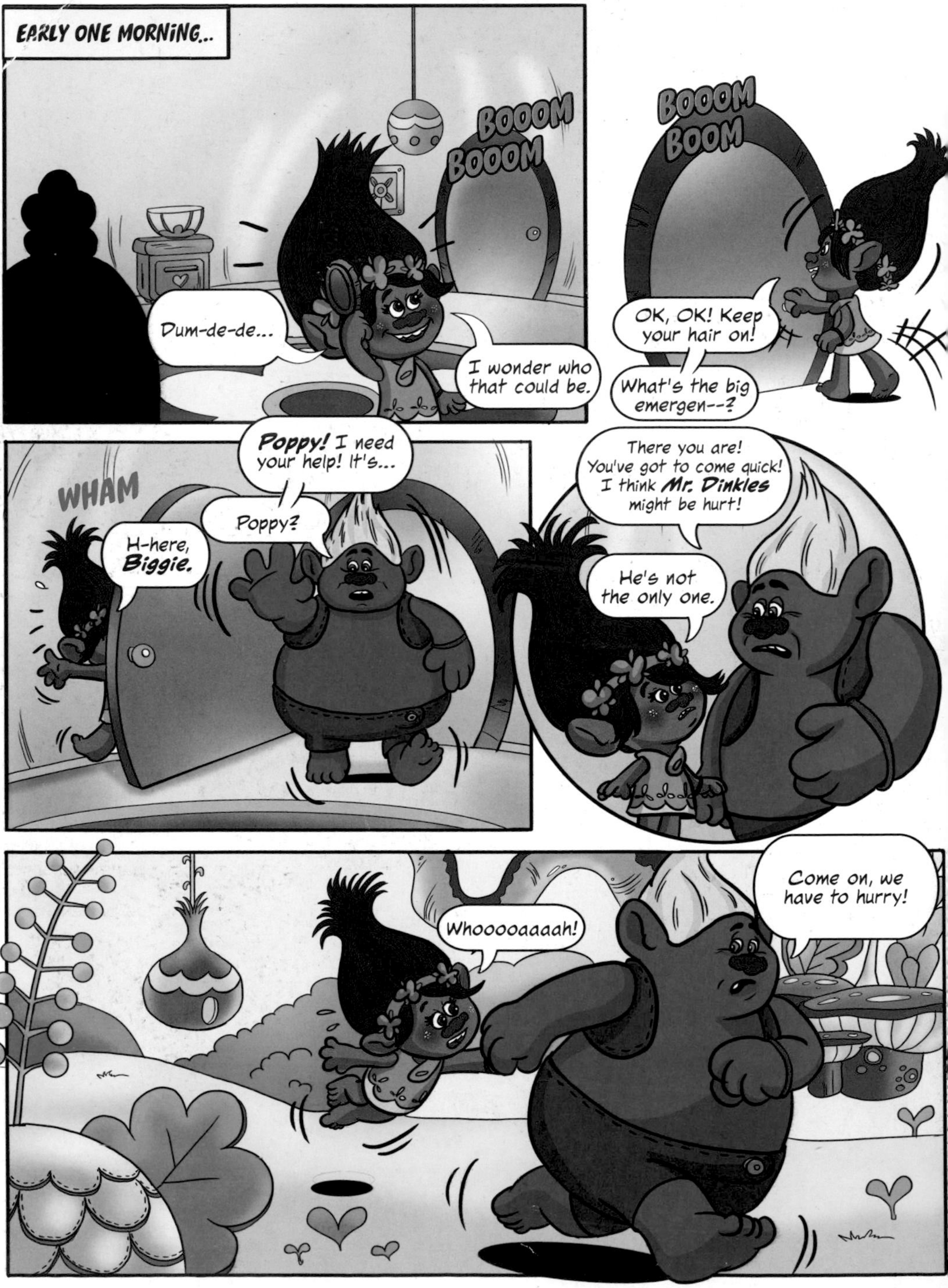

EARLY ONE MORNING...
BOOOM BOOOM
Dum-de-de...
I wonder who that could be.
BOOOM BOOM
OK, OK! Keep your hair on!
What's the big emergen--?
WHAM
Poppy! I need your help! It's...
Poppy?
H-here, Biggie.
There you are! You've got to come quick! I think Mr. Dinkles might be hurt!
He's not the only one.
Whoooaaaah!
Come on, we have to hurry!

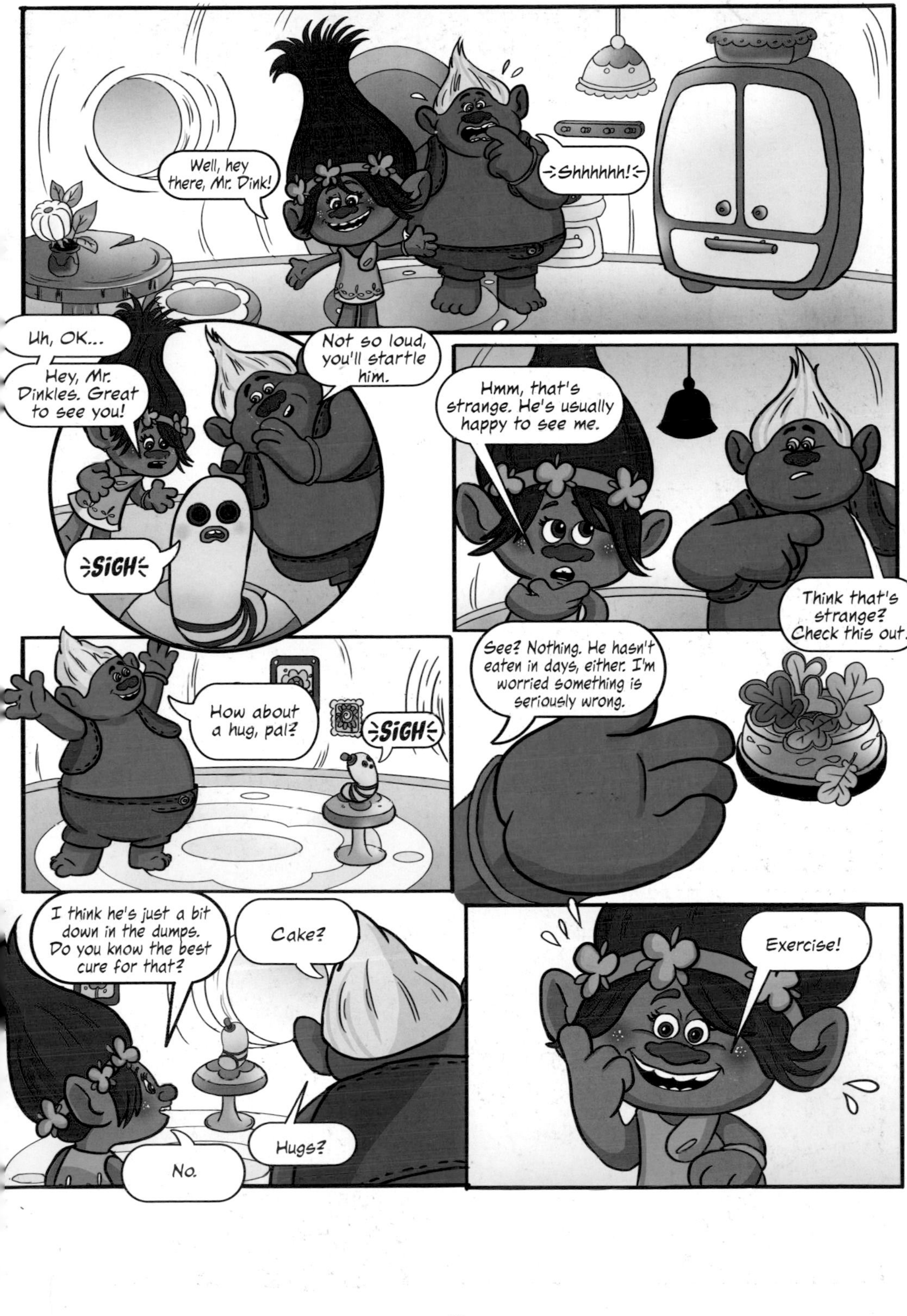

Well, hey there, Mr. Dink!
Shhhhhh!
Uh, OK...
Hey, Mr. Dinkles. Great to see you!
Not so loud, you'll startle him.
SIGH
Hmm, that's strange. He's usually happy to see me.
How about a hug, pal?
SIGH
Think that's strange? Check this out!
See? Nothing. He hasn't eaten in days, either. I'm worried something is seriously wrong.
I think he's just a bit down in the dumps. Do you know the best cure for that?
Cake?
No.
Hugs?
Exercise!

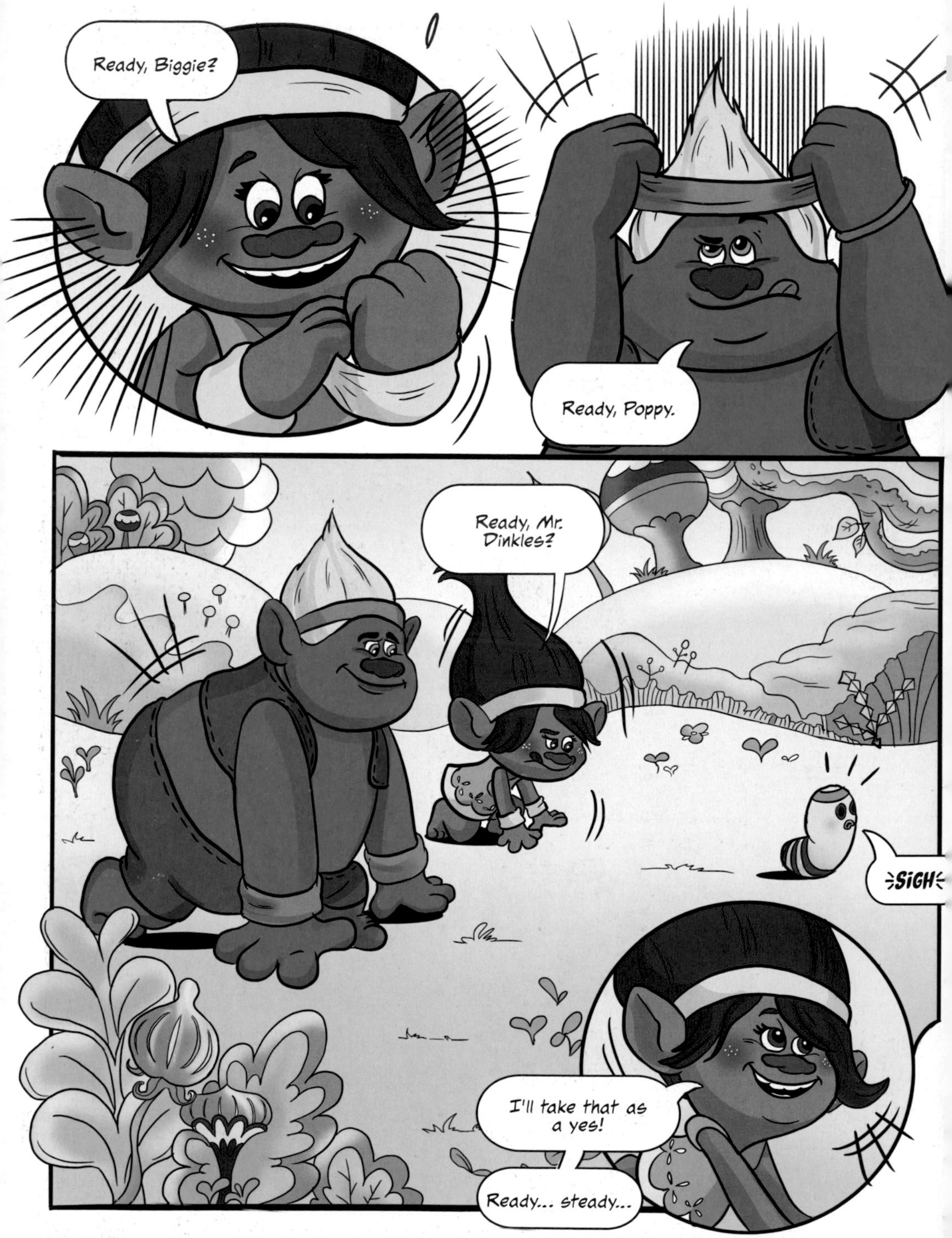

Ready, Biggie?
Ready, Poppy.
Ready, Mr. Dinkles?
SIGH
I'll take that as a yes!
Ready... steady...

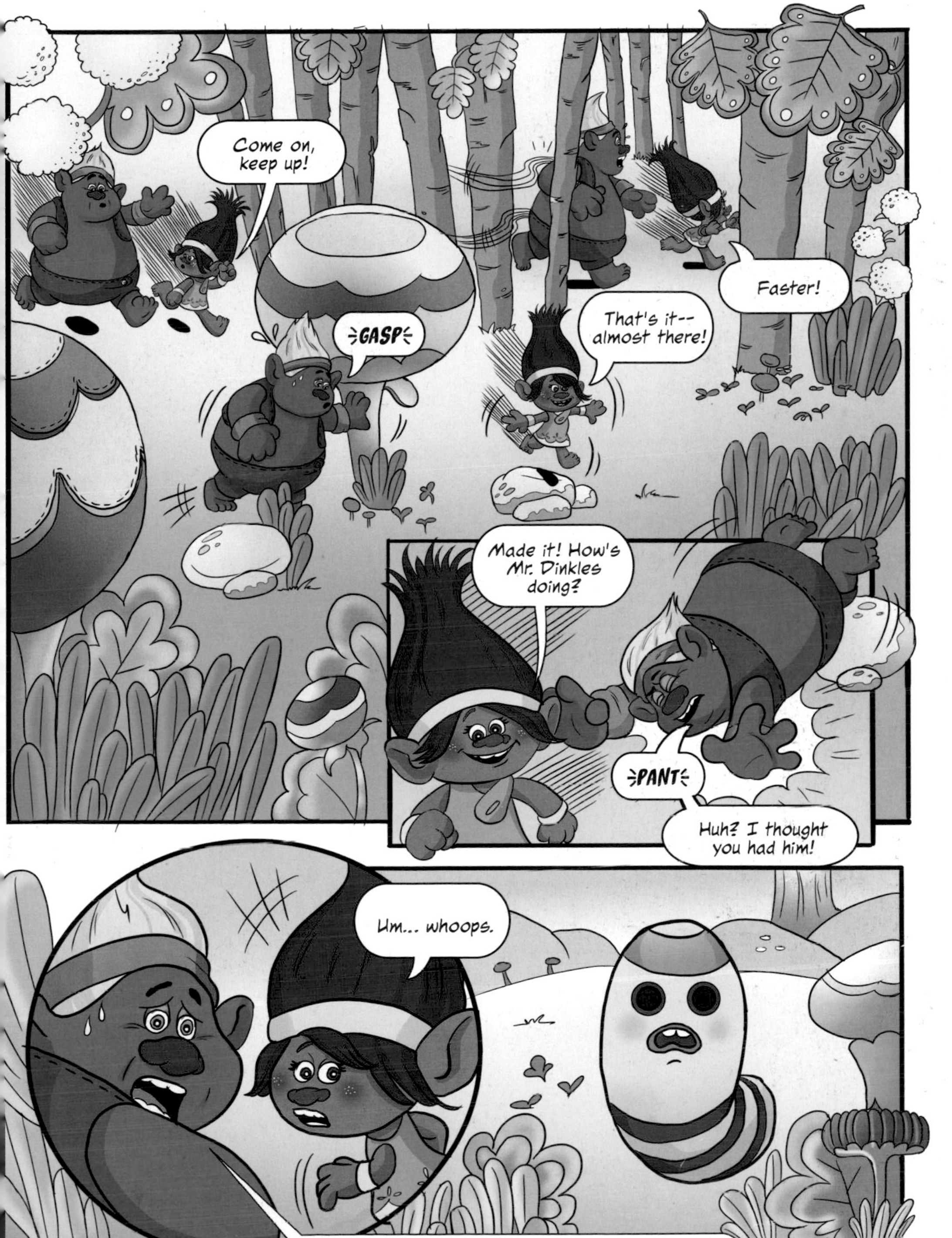
Come on, keep up!
GASP
That's it-- almost there!
Faster!
Made it! How's Mr. Dinkles doing?
PANT
Huh? I thought you had him!
Um... whoops.
Poor Mr. Dinkles... he's still at the starting line!

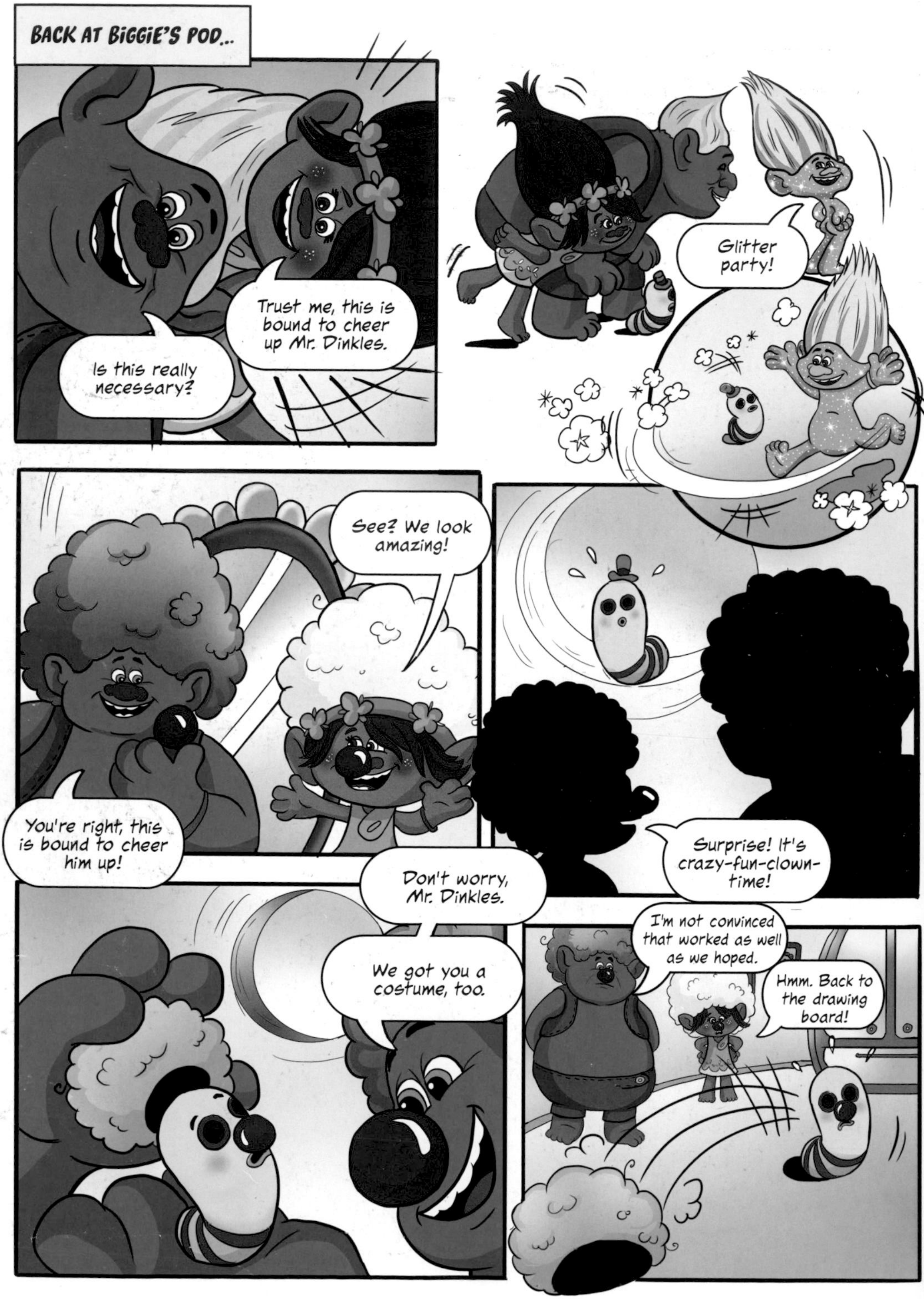
BACK AT BIGGIE'S POD...
Trust me, this is bound to cheer up Mr. Dinkles.
Is this really necessary?
Glitter party!
See? We look amazing!
You're right, this is bound to cheer him up!
Surprise! It's crazy-fun-clown-time!
Don't worry, Mr. Dinkles.
We got you a costume, too.
I'm not convinced that worked as well as we hoped.
Hmm. Back to the drawing board!

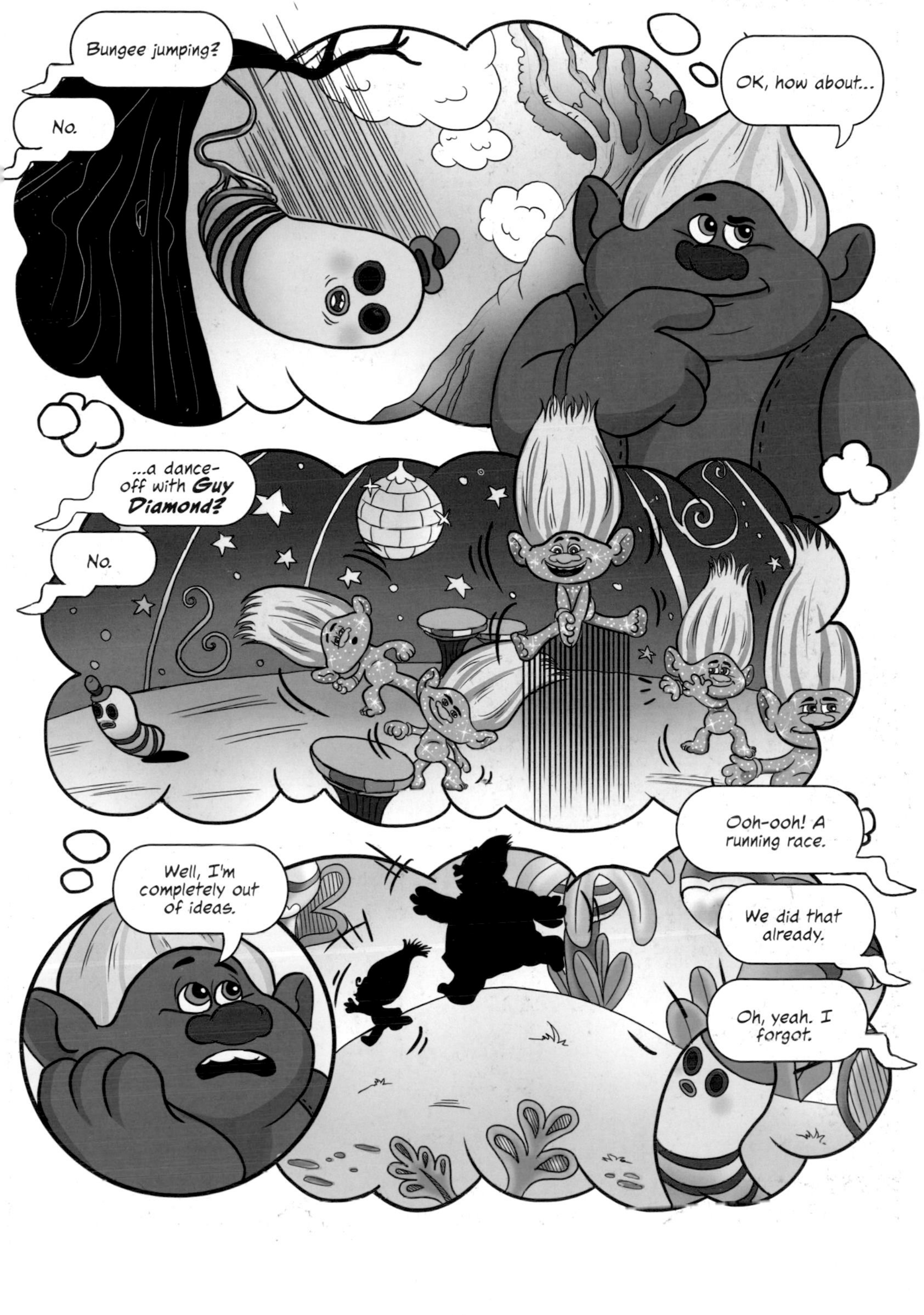
Bungee jumping?
No.
OK, how about...
...a dance-off with **Guy Diamond?**
No.
Well, I'm completely out of ideas.
Ooh-ooh! A running race.
We did that already.
Oh, yeah. I forgot.

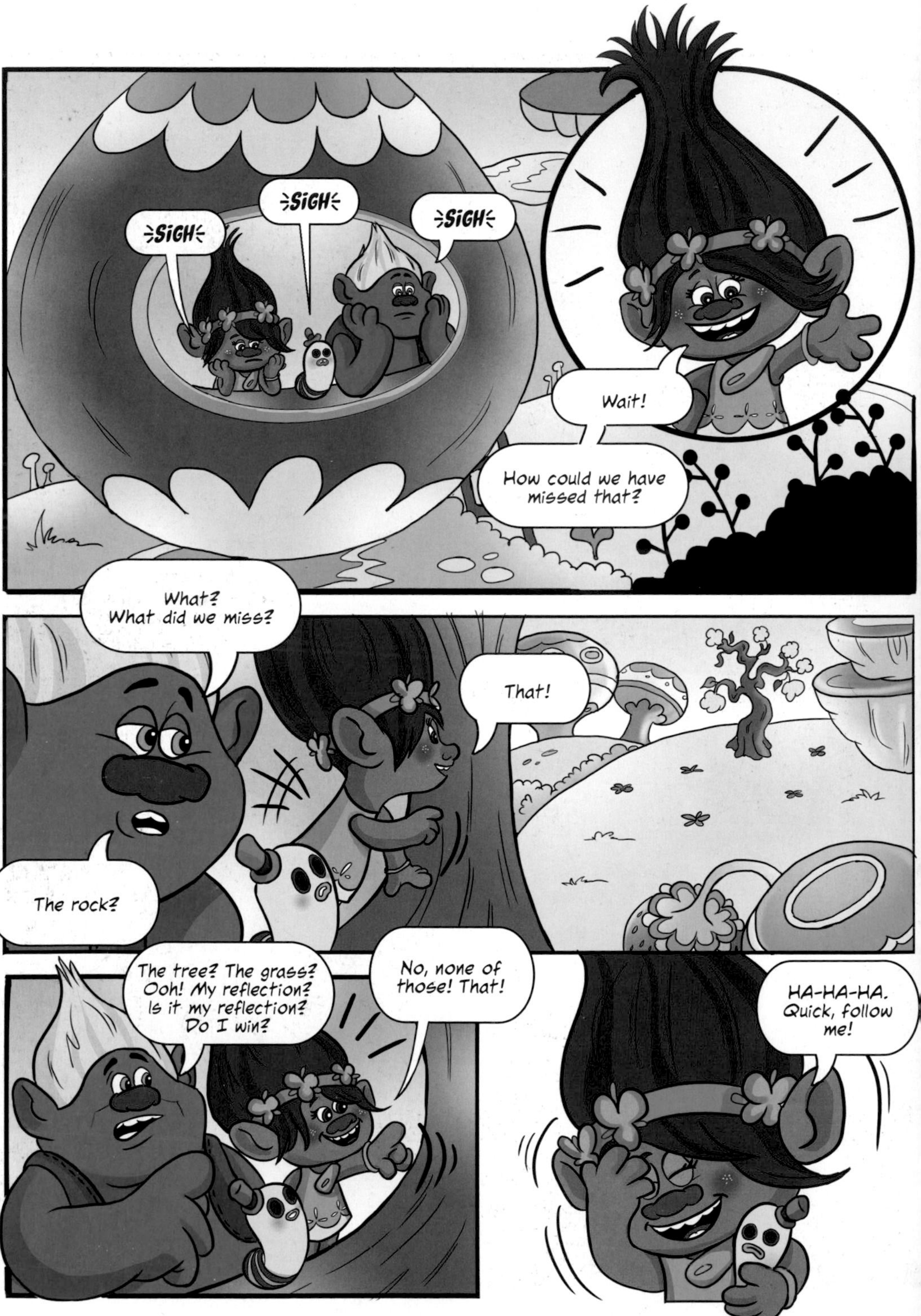

SIGH
SIGH
SIGH
Wait!
How could we have missed that?
What? What did we miss?
That!
The rock?
The tree? The grass? Ooh! My reflection? Is it my reflection? Do I win?
No, none of those! That!
HA-HA-HA. Quick, follow me!

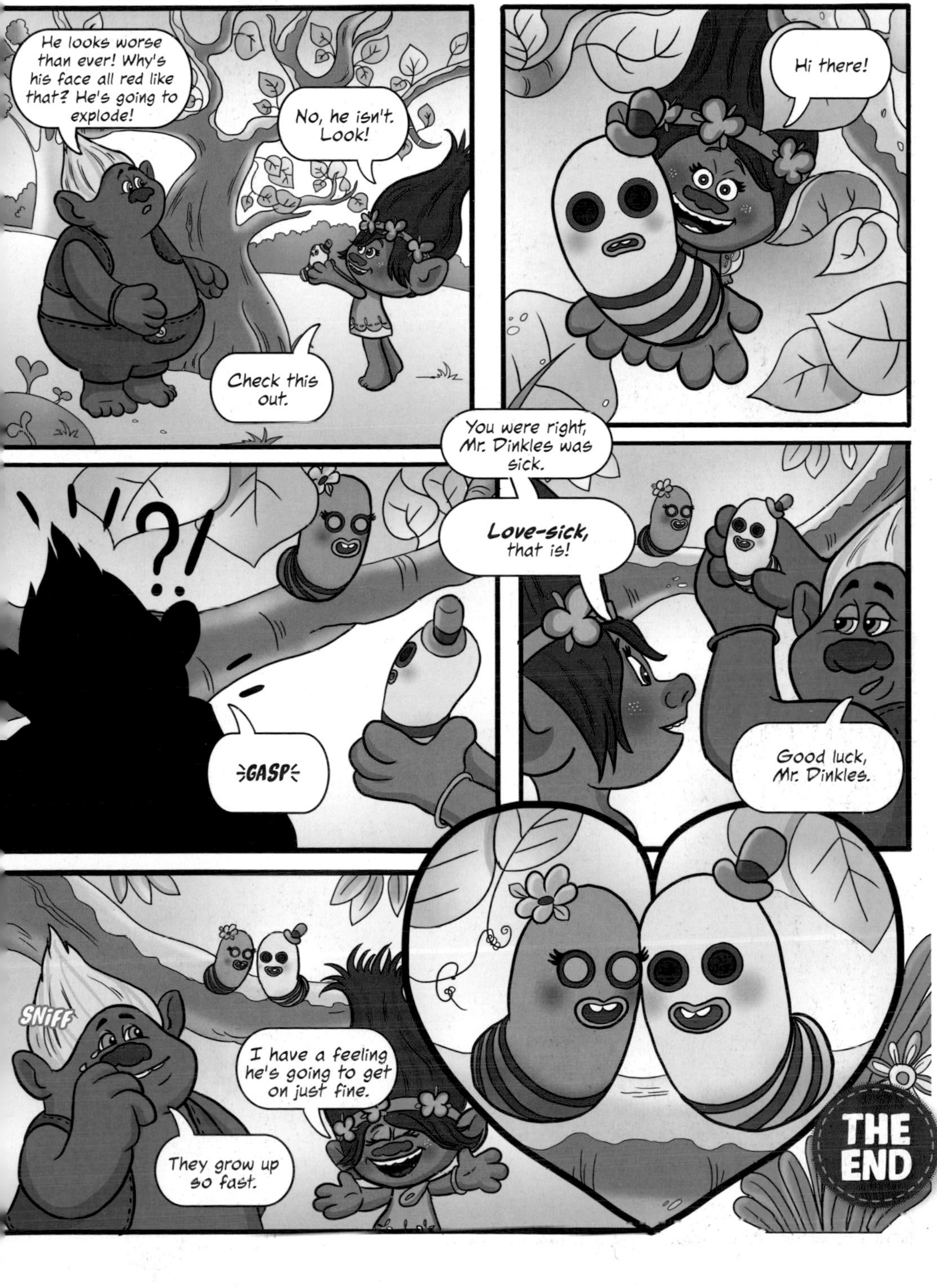
He looks worse than ever! Why's his face all red like that? He's going to explode!
No, he isn't. Look!
Check this out.
Hi there!
?!
GASP
You were right, Mr. Dinkles was sick.
Love-sick, that is!
Good luck, Mr. Dinkles.
SNIFF
I have a feeling he's going to get on just fine.
They grow up so fast.
THE END

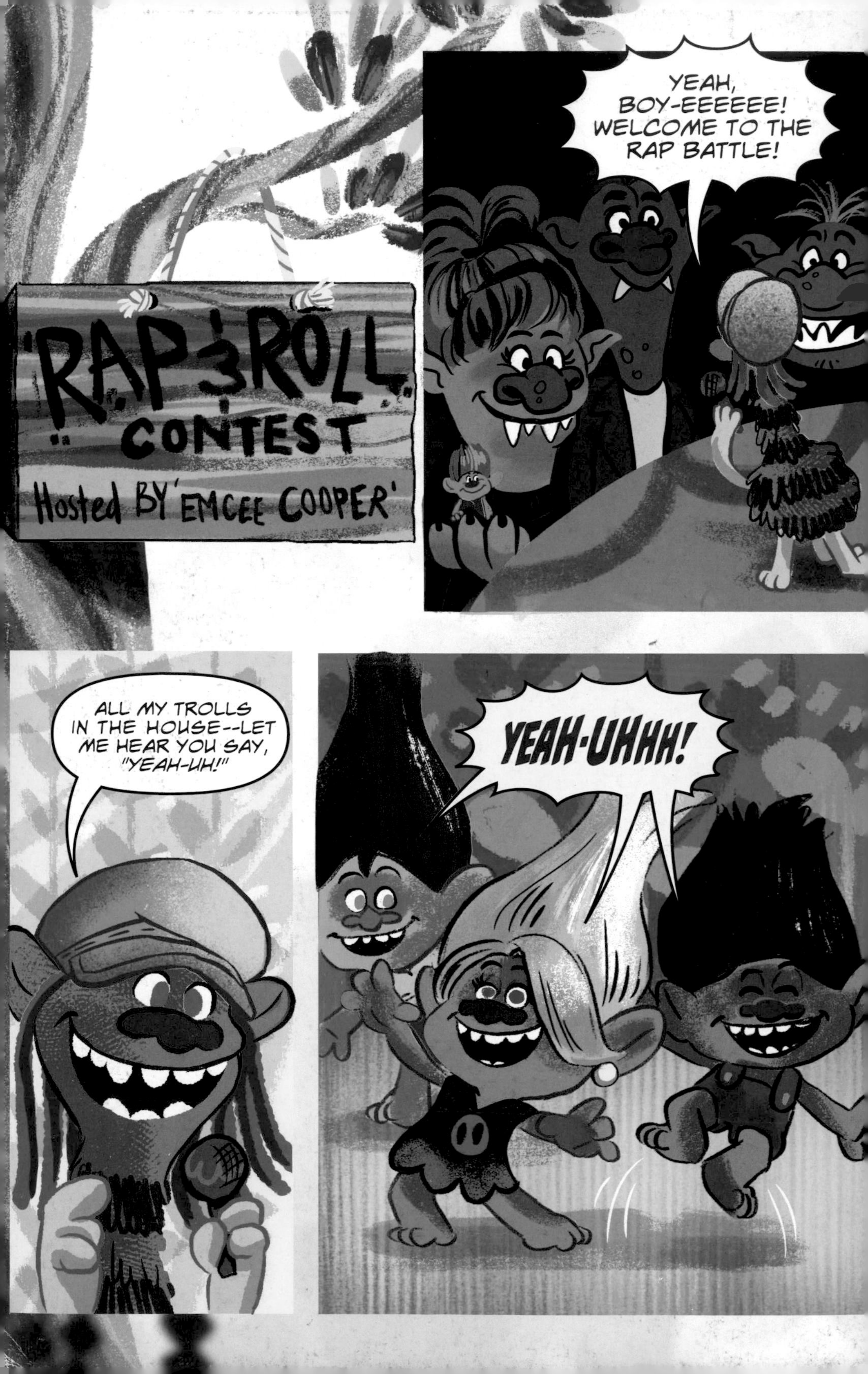
RAP 3 ROLL CONTEST
Hosted BY 'EMCEE COOPER'
YEAH, BOY-EEEEEE! WELCOME TO THE RAP BATTLE!
ALL MY TROLLS IN THE HOUSE--LET ME HEAR YOU SAY, "YEAH-UH!"
YEAH-UHHH!

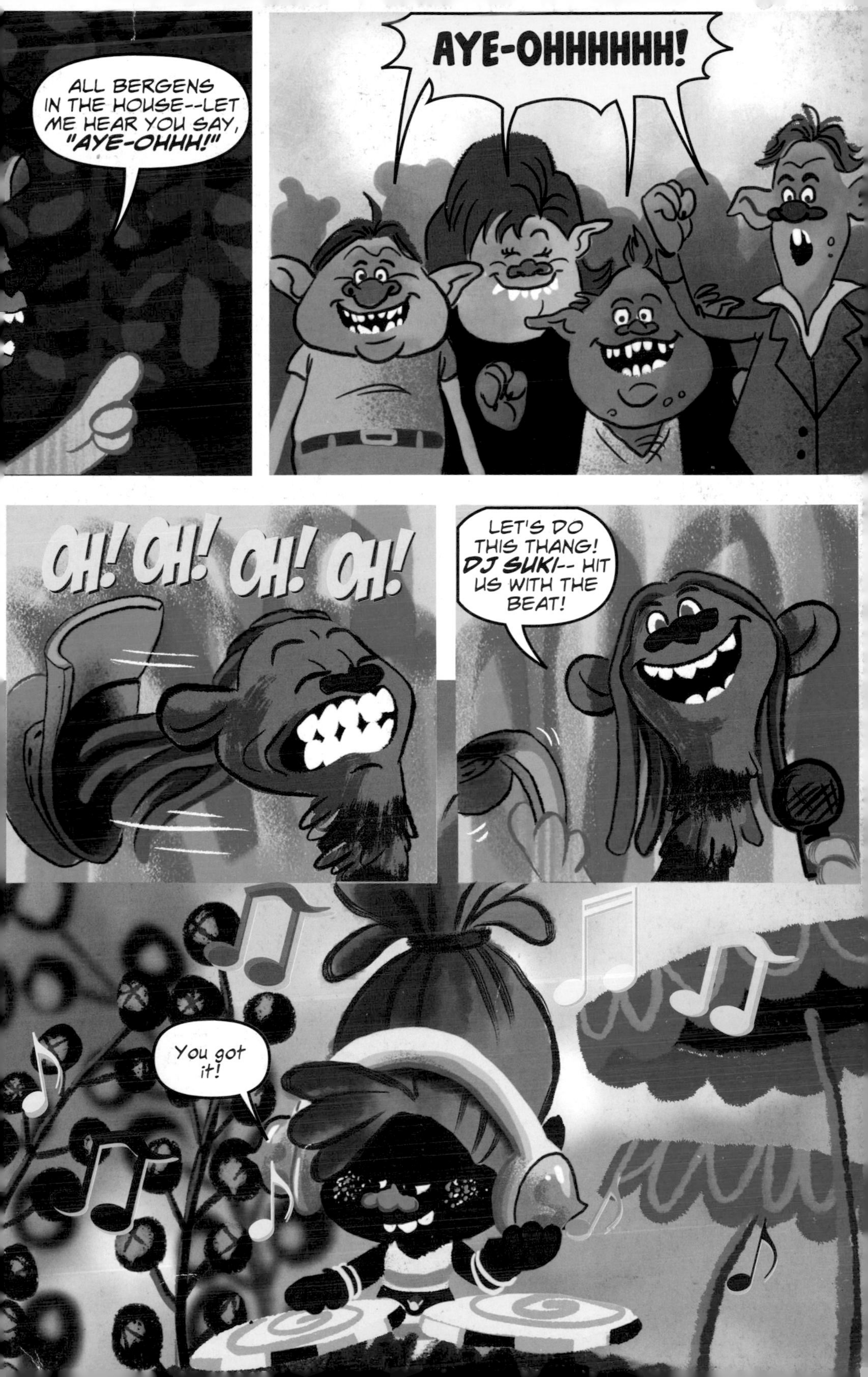

ALL BERGENS IN THE HOUSE--LET ME HEAR YOU SAY, *"AYE-OHHH!"*
AYE-OHHHHHH!
OH! OH! OH! OH!
LET'S DO THIS THANG! ***DJ SUKI***-- HIT US WITH THE BEAT!
You got it!

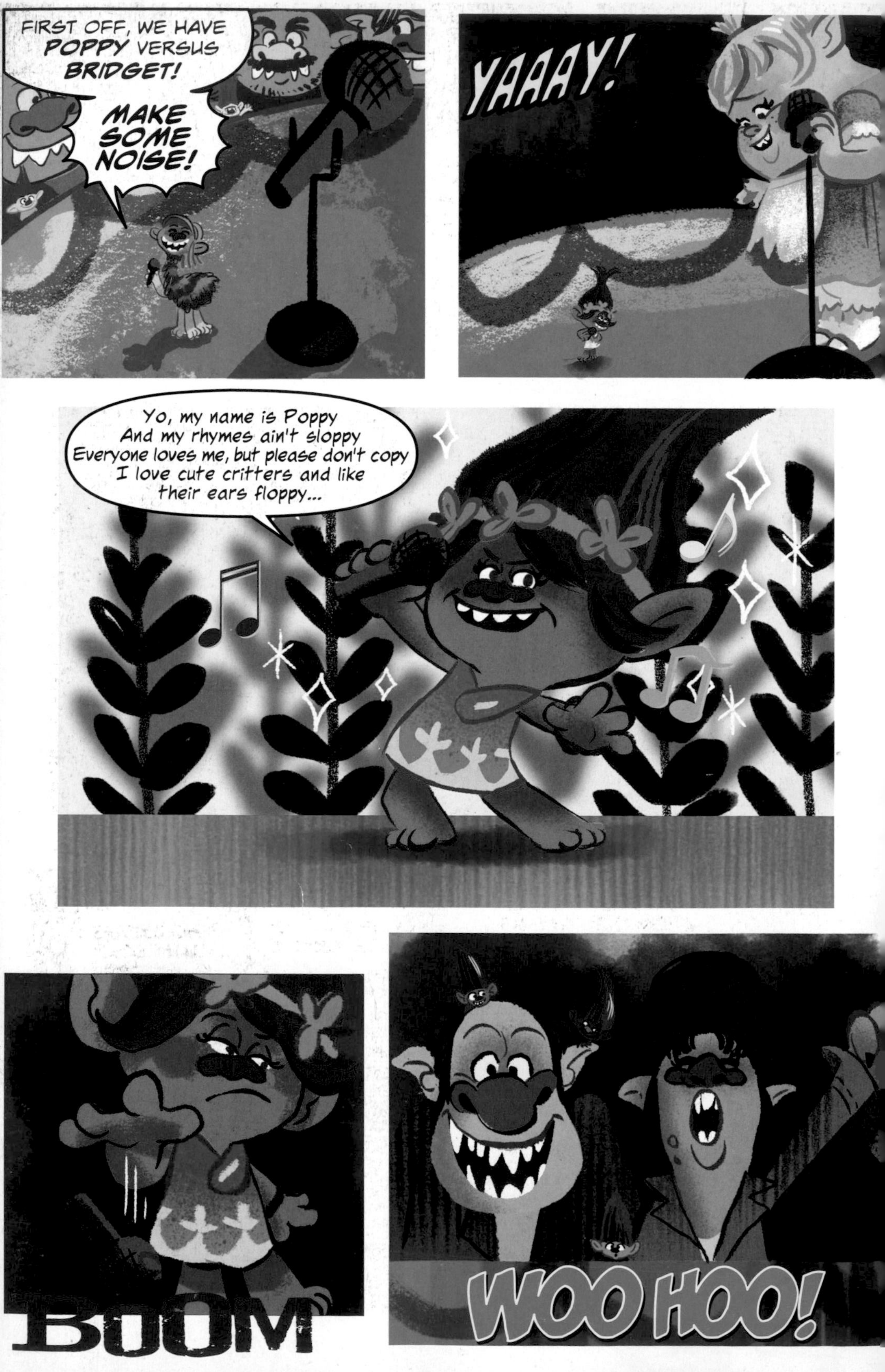
FIRST OFF, WE HAVE POPPY VERSUS BRIDGET!
MAKE SOME NOISE!
YAAAY!
Yo, my name is Poppy
And my rhymes ain't sloppy
Everyone loves me, but please don't copy
I love cute critters and like
their ears floppy...
BOOM
WOO HOO!

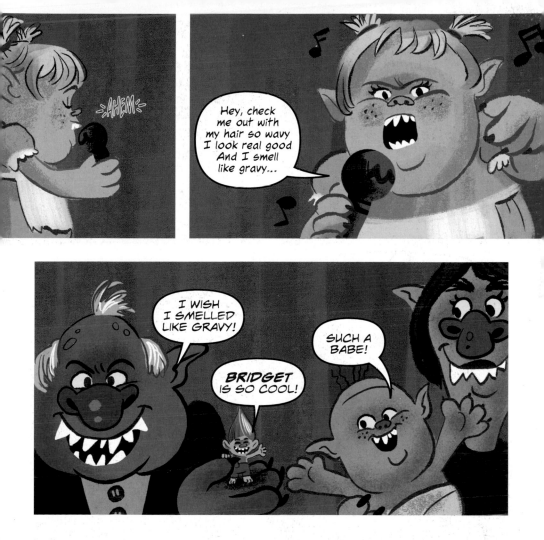

AHEM

Hey, check me out with my hair so wavy I look real good And I smell like gravy...

I WISH I SMELLED LIKE GRAVY!

BRIDGET IS SO COOL!

SUCH A BABE!

NOW FOR THE MAIN EVENT--*KING GRISTLE* VERSUS *BRANCH!*

THIS IS GOING TO BE CRAZY!

I'M SO EXCITED, I CAN'T STOP *SMILING!*

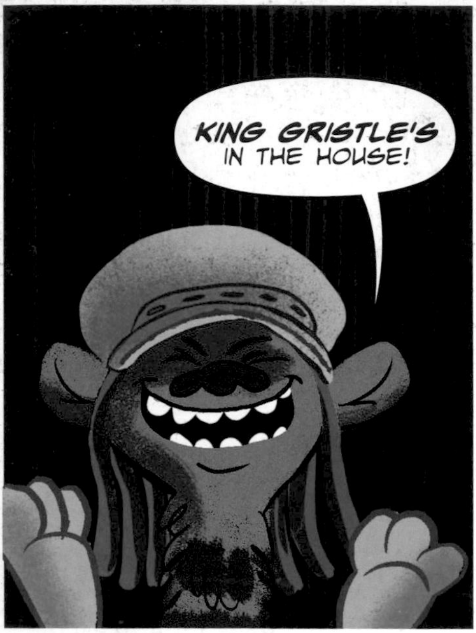
KING GRISTLE'S IN THE HOUSE!

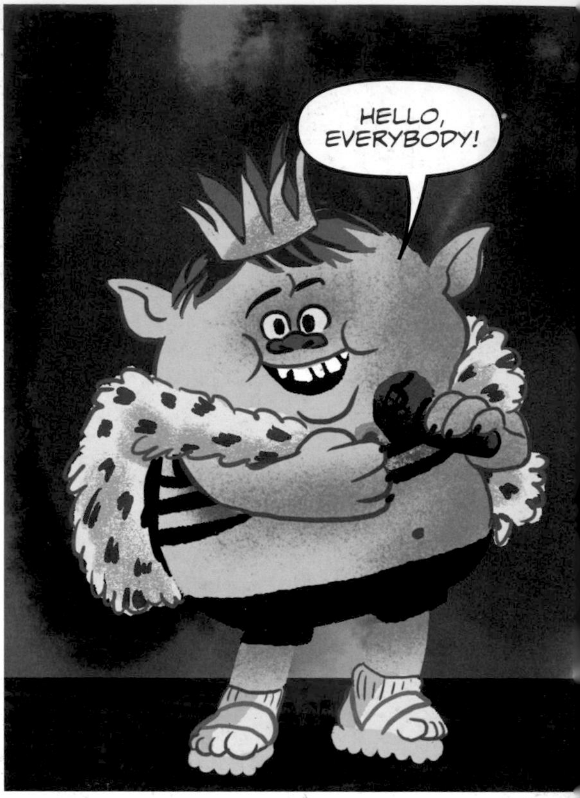
HELLO, EVERYBODY!

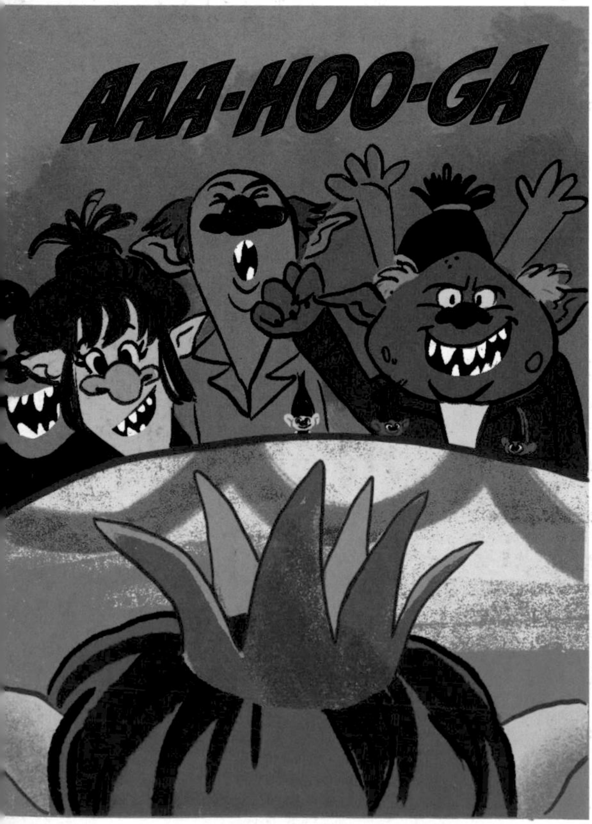
AAA-HOO-GA

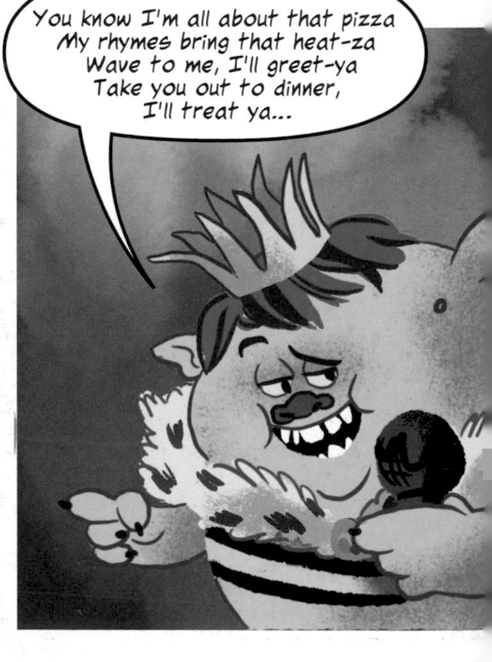
You know I'm all about that pizza
My rhymes bring that heat-za
Wave to me, I'll greet-ya
Take you out to dinner,
I'll treat ya...

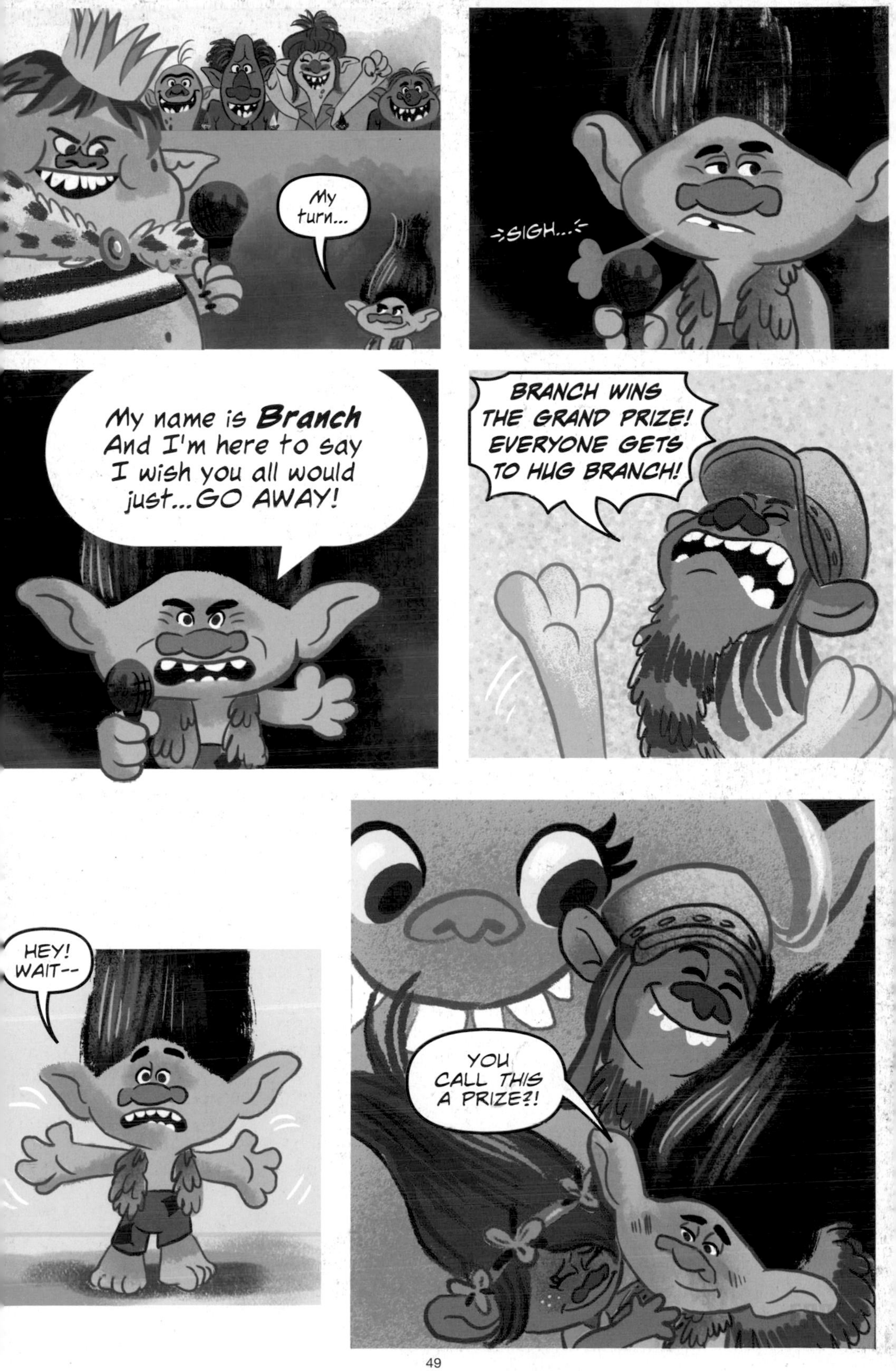
My turn...
SIGH...
My name is Branch And I'm here to say I wish you all would just...GO AWAY!
BRANCH WINS THE GRAND PRIZE! EVERYONE GETS TO HUG BRANCH!
HEY! WAIT--
YOU CALL THIS A PRIZE?!

ALONG CAME A SPIDER

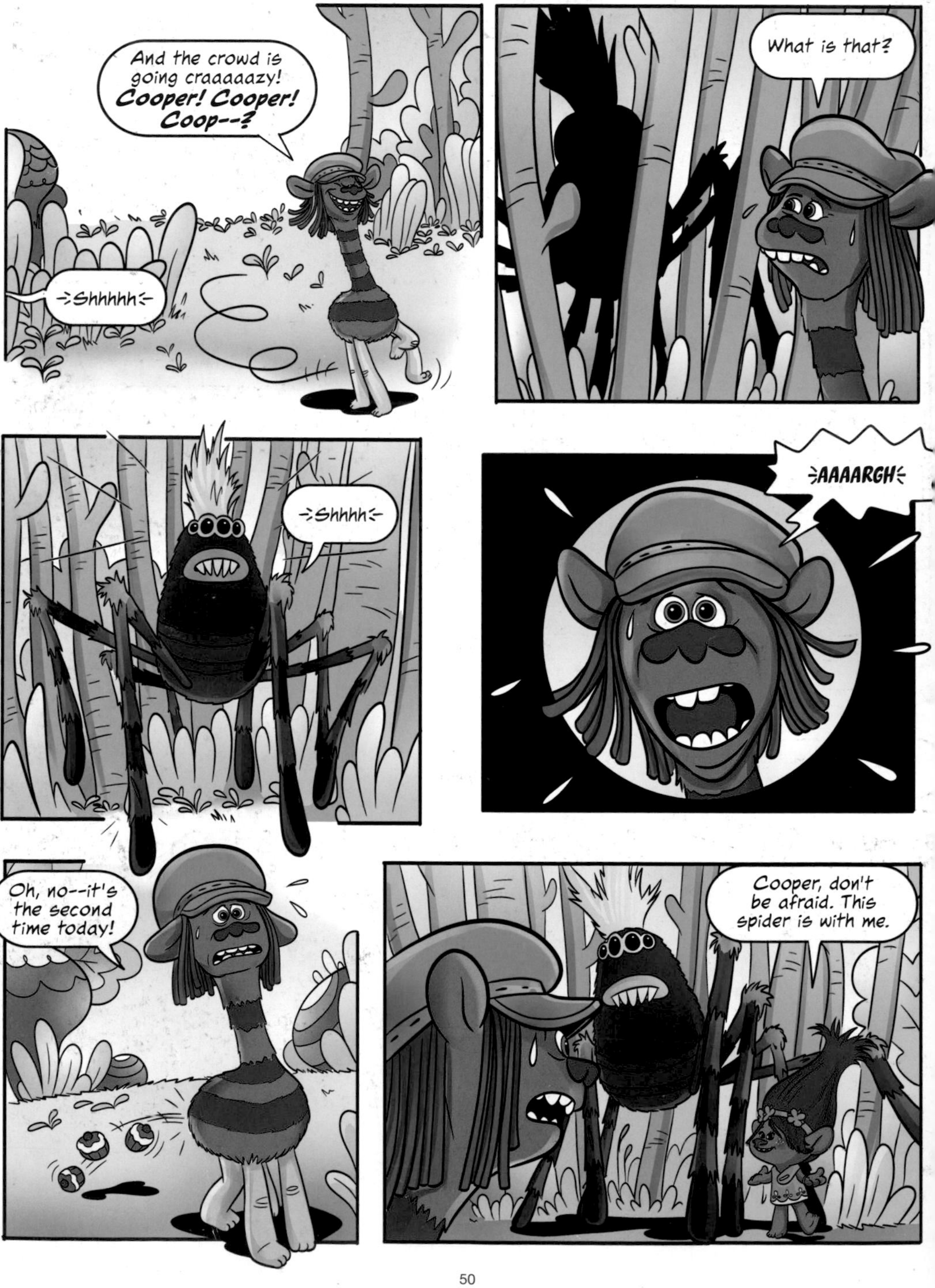

And the crowd is going craaaaazy! **Cooper! Cooper! Coop--?**
Shhhhh
What is that?
Shhhh
AAAARGH
Oh, no--it's the second time today!
Cooper, don't be afraid. This spider is with me.

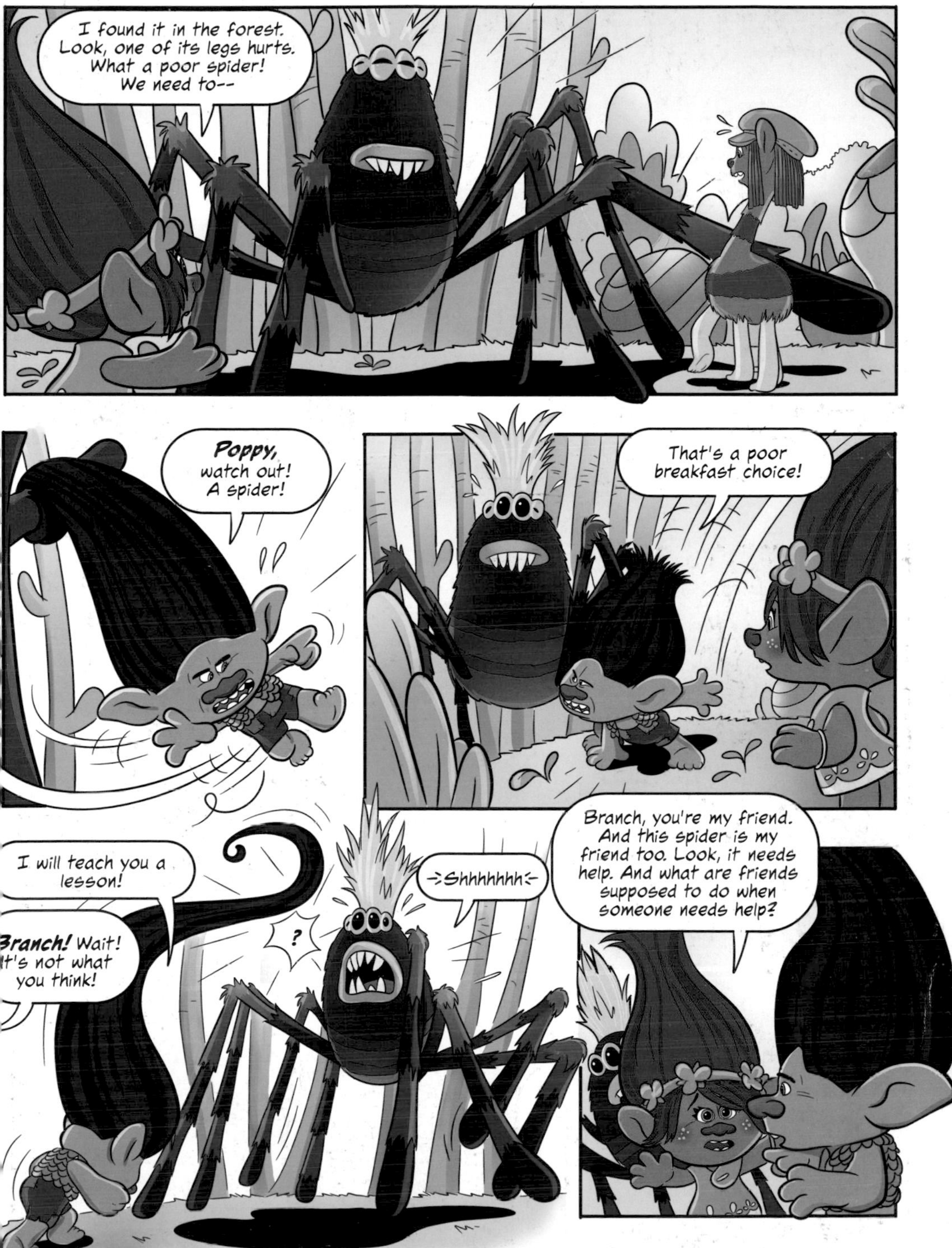
I found it in the forest. Look, one of its legs hurts. What a poor spider! We need to--
Poppy, watch out! A spider!
That's a poor breakfast choice!
I will teach you a lesson!
Branch! Wait! It's not what you think!
?
Shhhhhhh
Branch, you're my friend. And this spider is my friend too. Look, it needs help. And what are friends supposed to do when someone needs help?

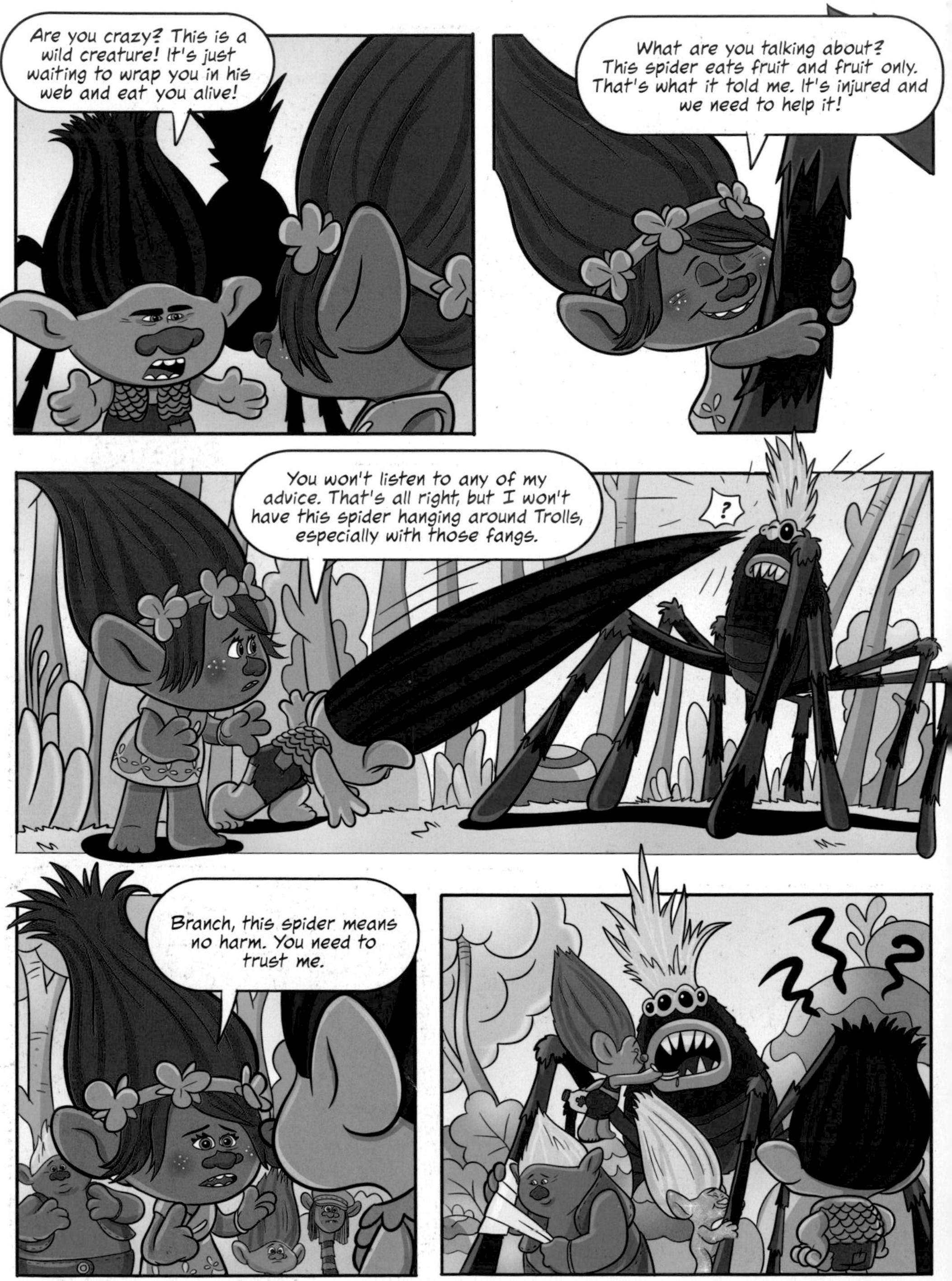
Are you crazy? This is a wild creature! It's just waiting to wrap you in his web and eat you alive!
What are you talking about? This spider eats fruit and fruit only. That's what it told me. It's injured and we need to help it!
You won't listen to any of my advice. That's all right, but I won't have this spider hanging around Trolls, especially with those fangs.
?
Branch, this spider means no harm. You need to trust me.

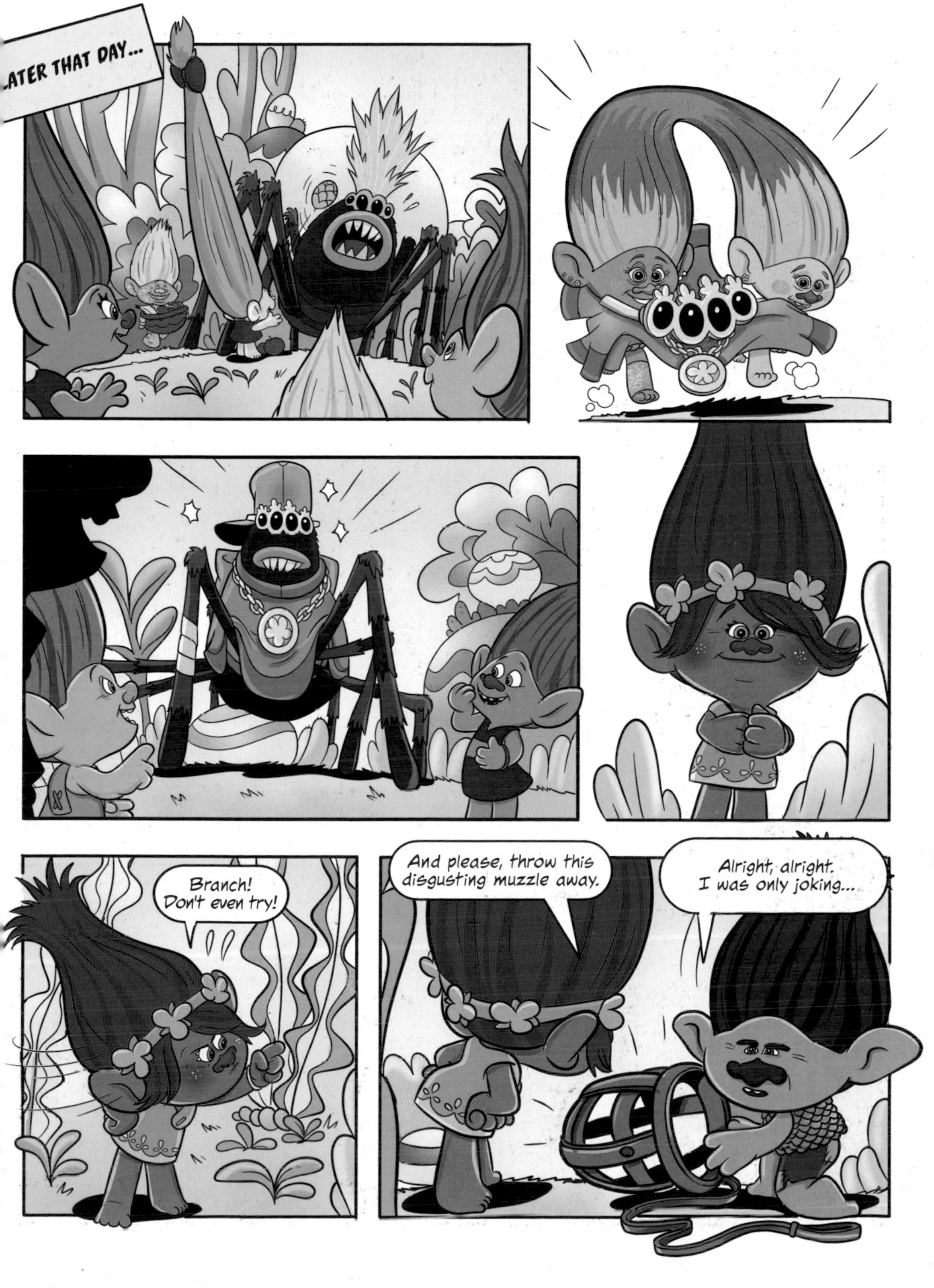

LATER THAT DAY...
Branch! Don't even try!
And please, throw this disgusting muzzle away.
Alright, alright. I was only joking...

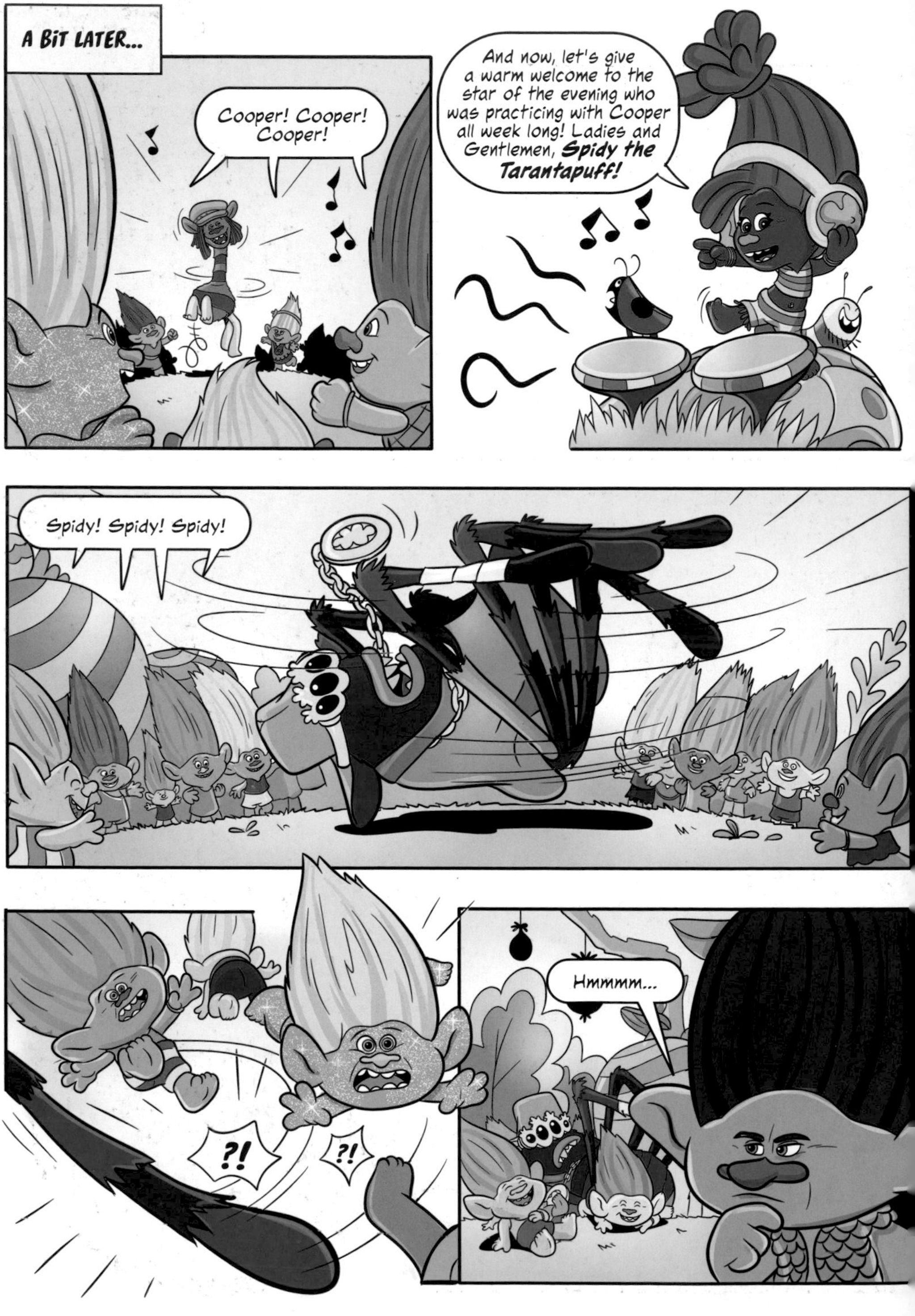
A BIT LATER...
Cooper! Cooper! Cooper!
And now, let's give a warm welcome to the star of the evening who was practicing with Cooper all week long! Ladies and Gentlemen, **Spidy the Tarantapuff!**
Spidy! Spidy! Spidy!
?!
?!
Hmmmm...

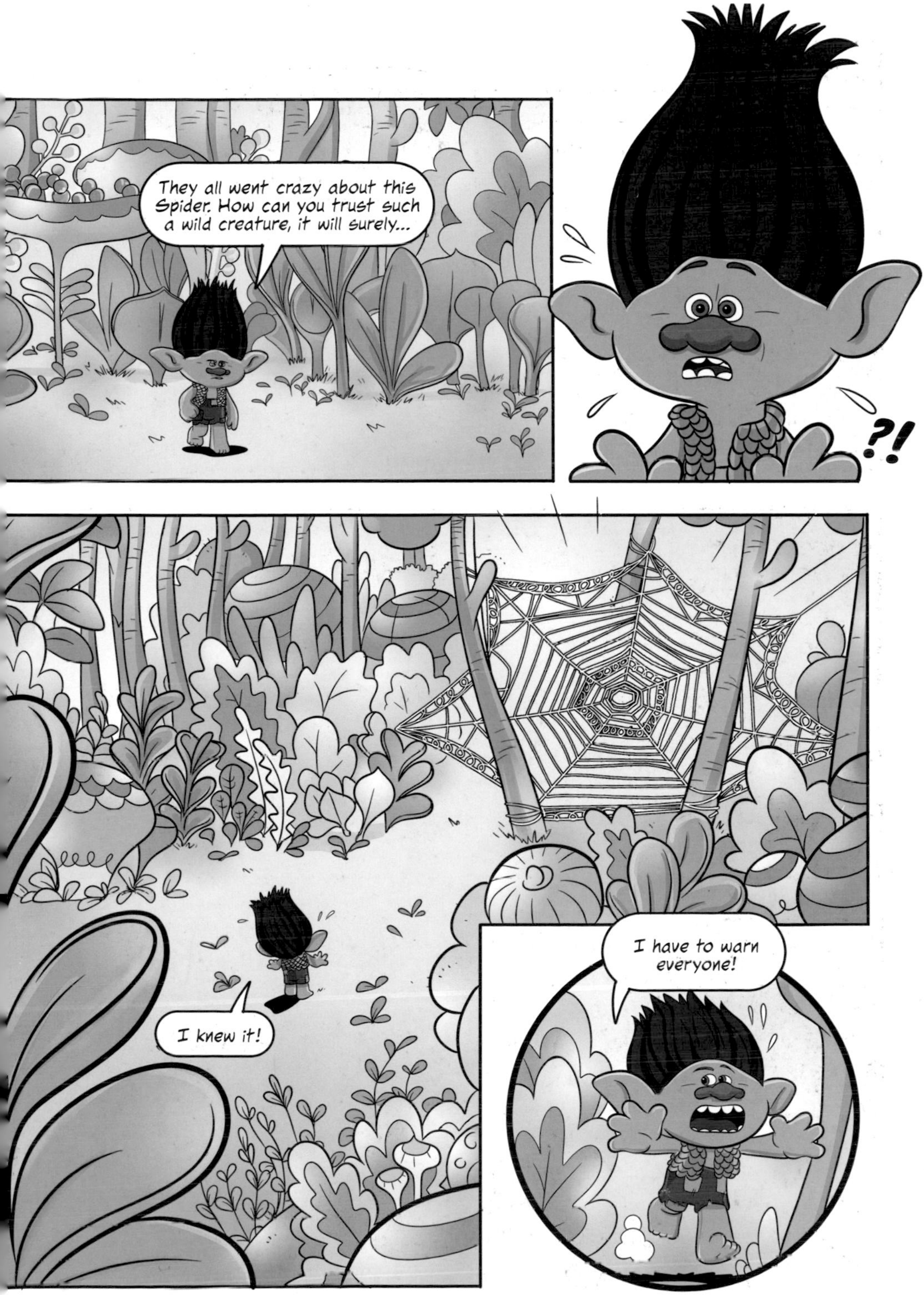
They all went crazy about this Spider. How can you trust such a wild creature, it will surely...
?!
I knew it!
I have to warn everyone!

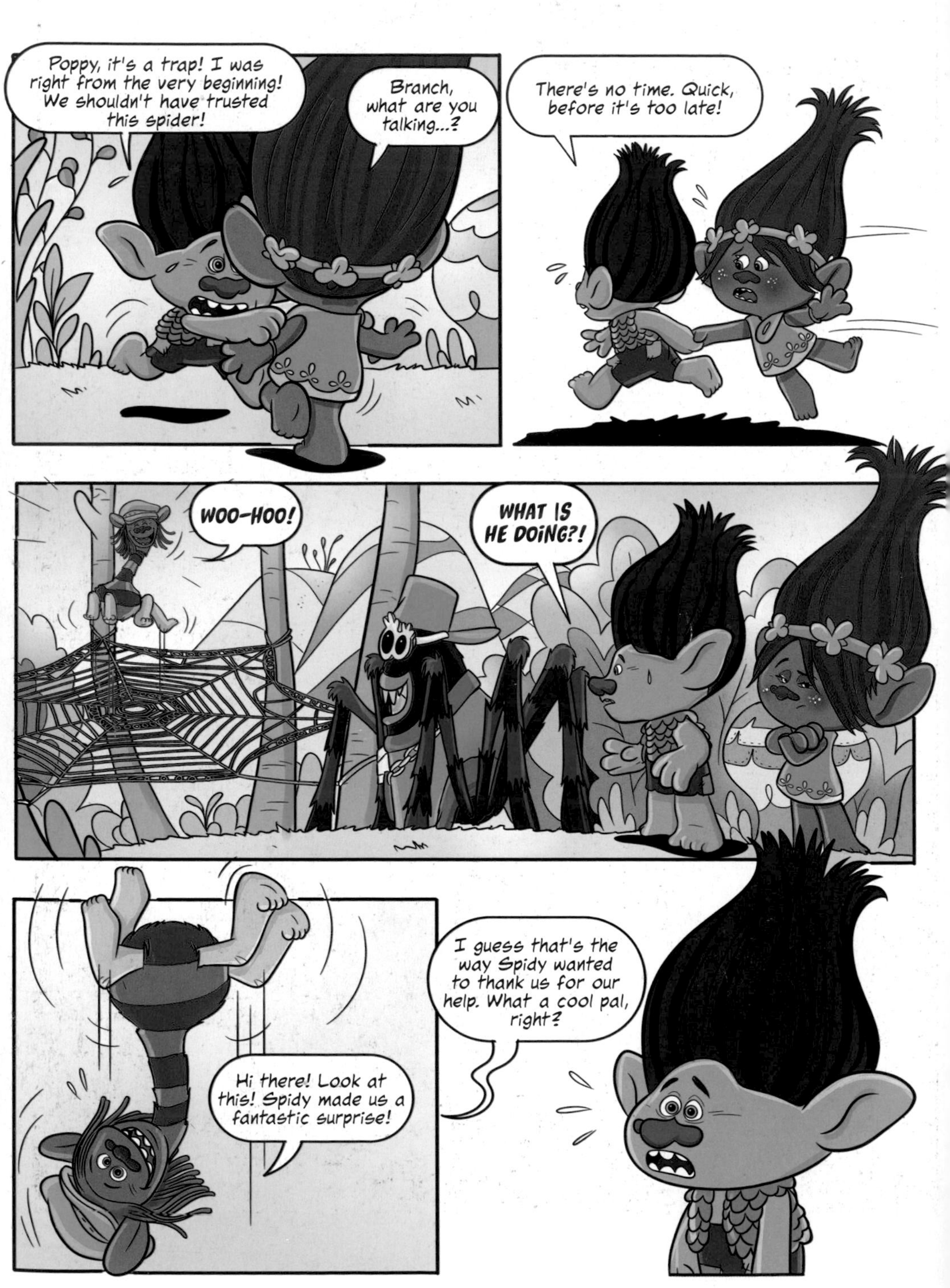
Poppy, it's a trap! I was right from the very beginning! We shouldn't have trusted this spider!
Branch, what are you talking...?
There's no time. Quick, before it's too late!
WOO-HOO!
WHAT IS HE DOING?!
Hi there! Look at this! Spidy made us a fantastic surprise!
I guess that's the way Spidy wanted to thank us for our help. What a cool pal, right?

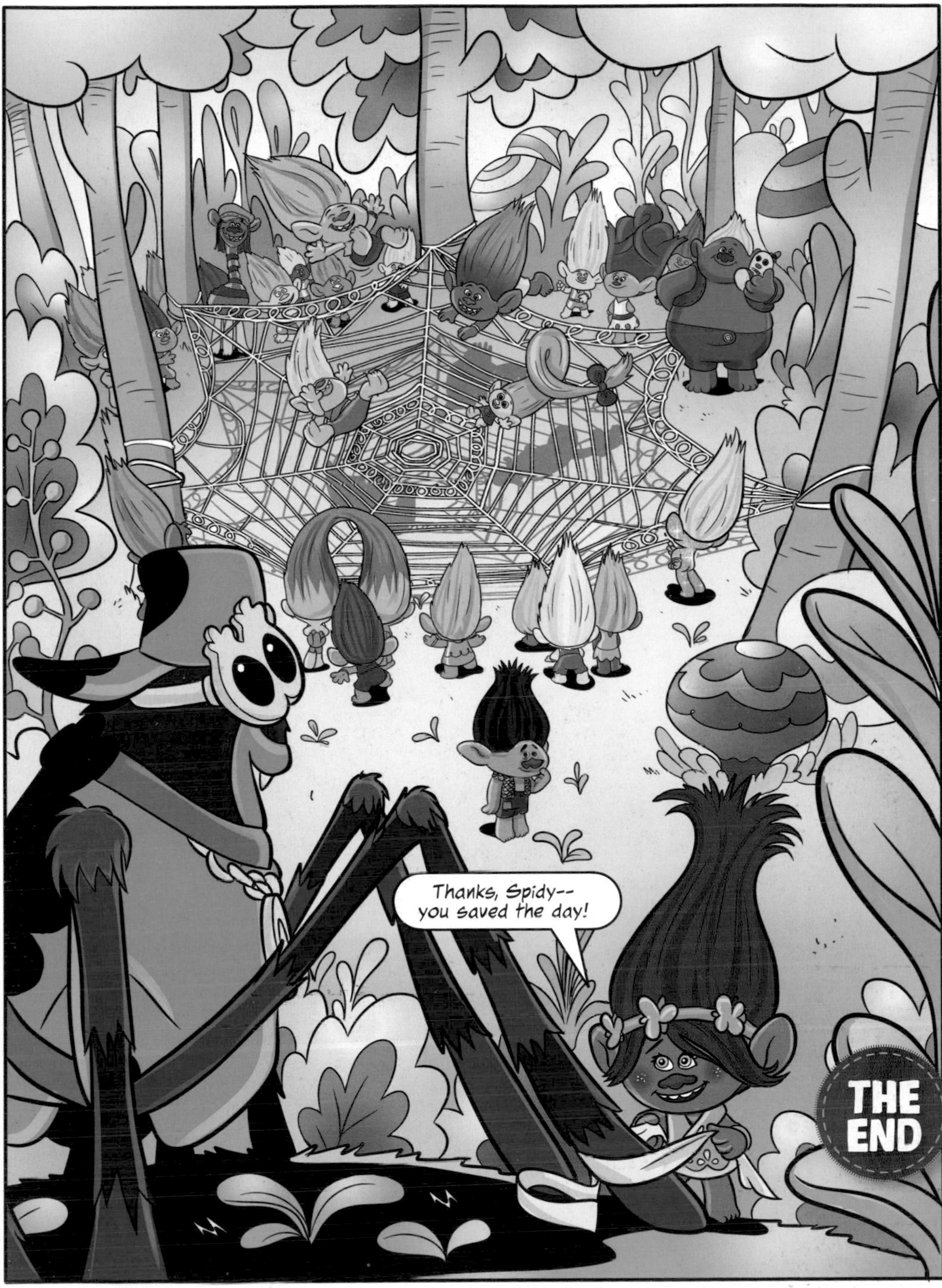
Thanks, Spidy--
you saved the day!
THE END

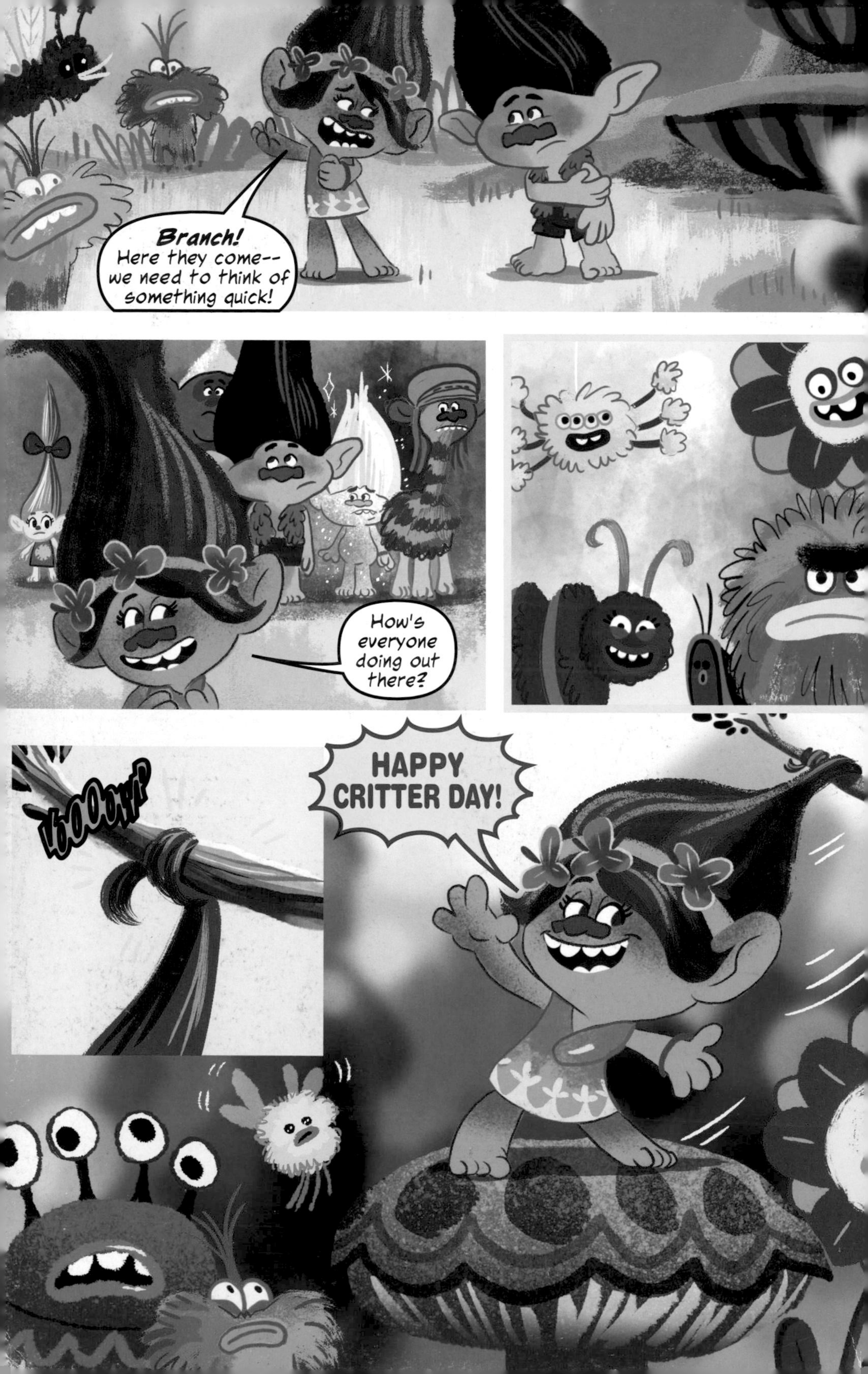
Branch!
Here they come--
we need to think of
something quick!
How's everyone doing out there?
HAPPY CRITTER DAY!

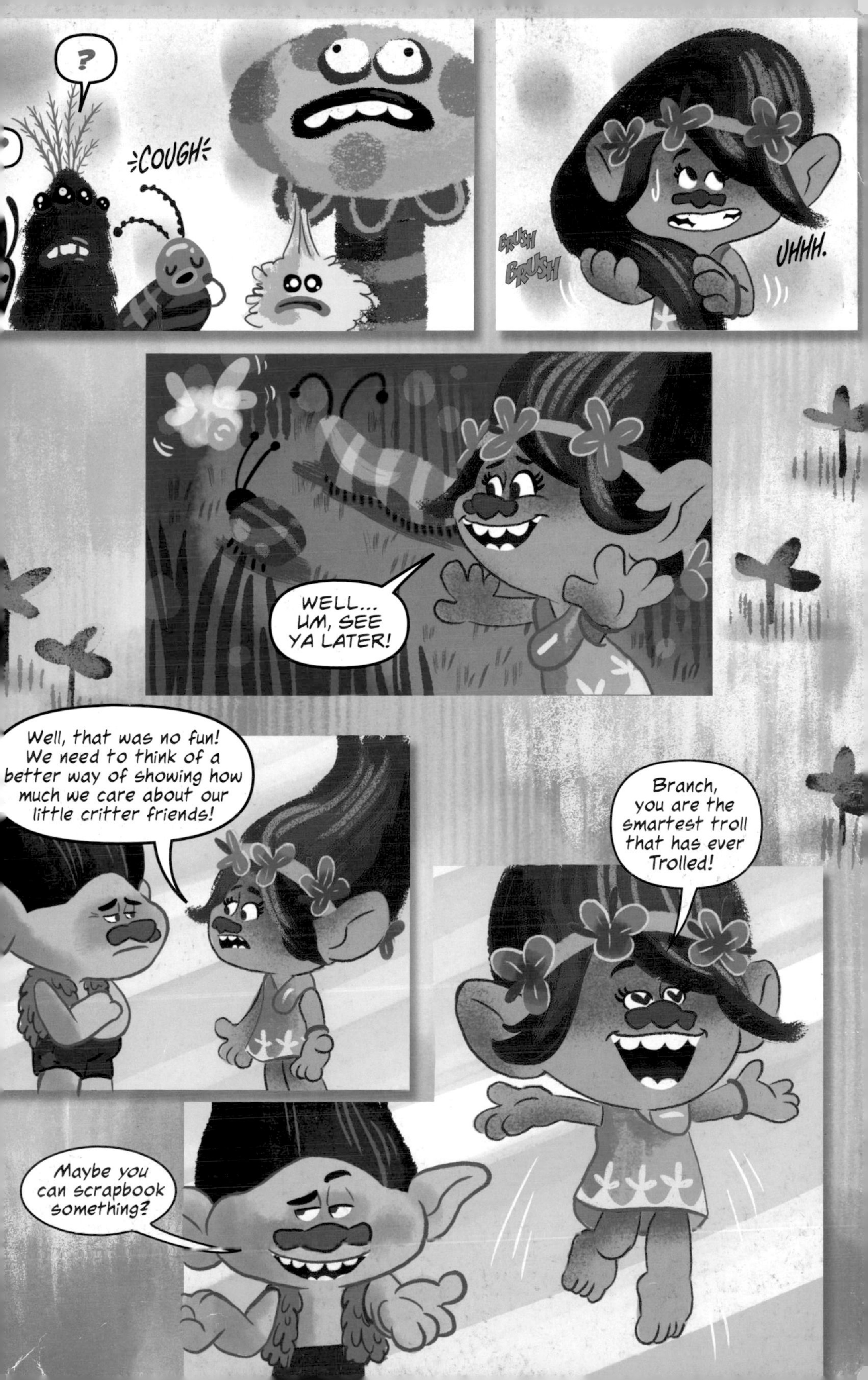
?
COUGH
BRUSH
BRUSH
UHHH.
WELL... UM, SEE YA LATER!
Well, that was no fun! We need to think of a better way of showing how much we care about our little critter friends!
Branch, you are the smartest troll that has ever Trolled!
Maybe you can scrapbook something?

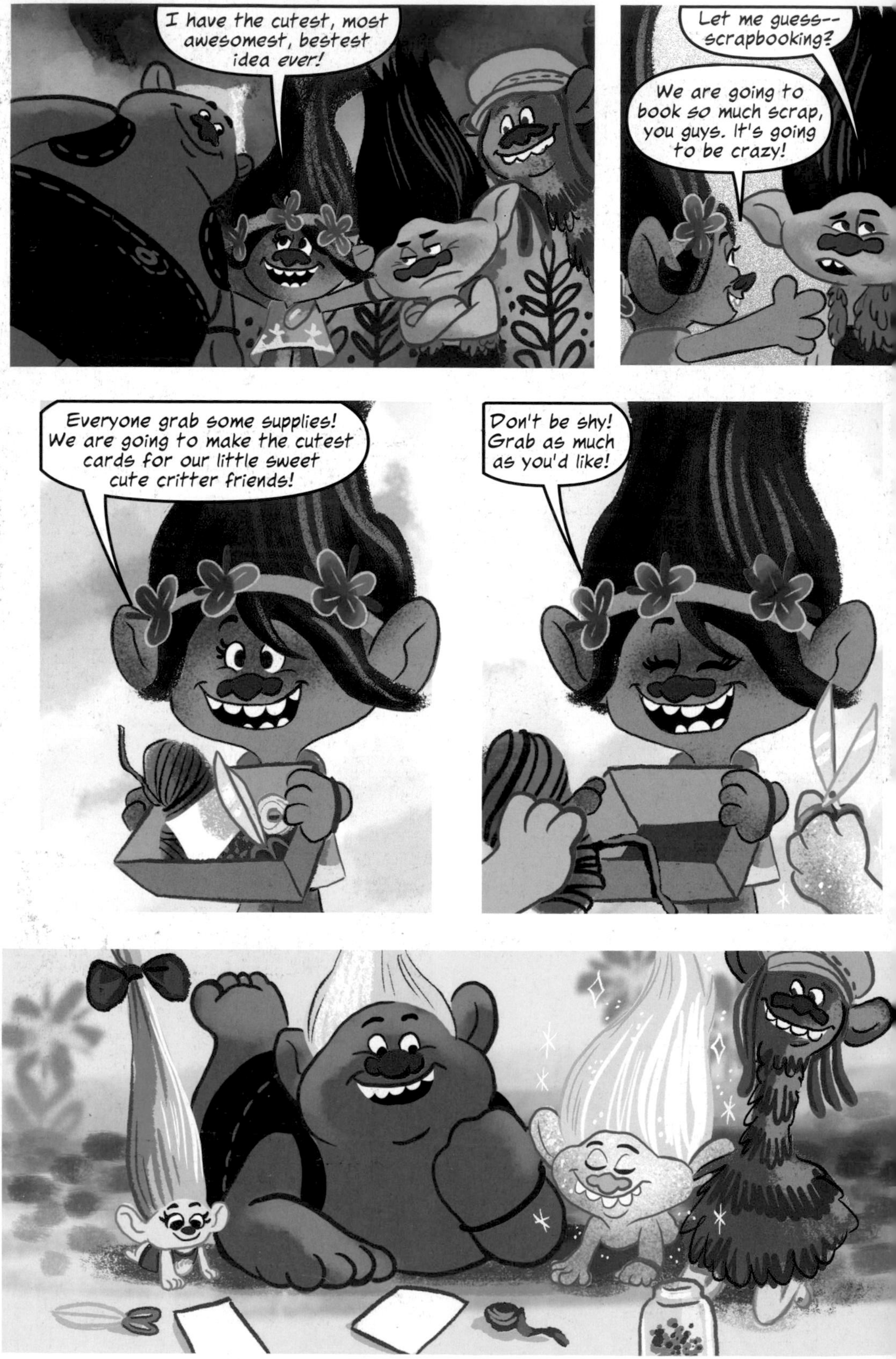
I have the cutest, most awesomest, bestest idea ever!
Let me guess--scrapbooking?
We are going to book so much scrap, you guys. It's going to be crazy!
Everyone grab some supplies! We are going to make the cutest cards for our little sweet cute critter friends!
Don't be shy! Grab as much as you'd like!

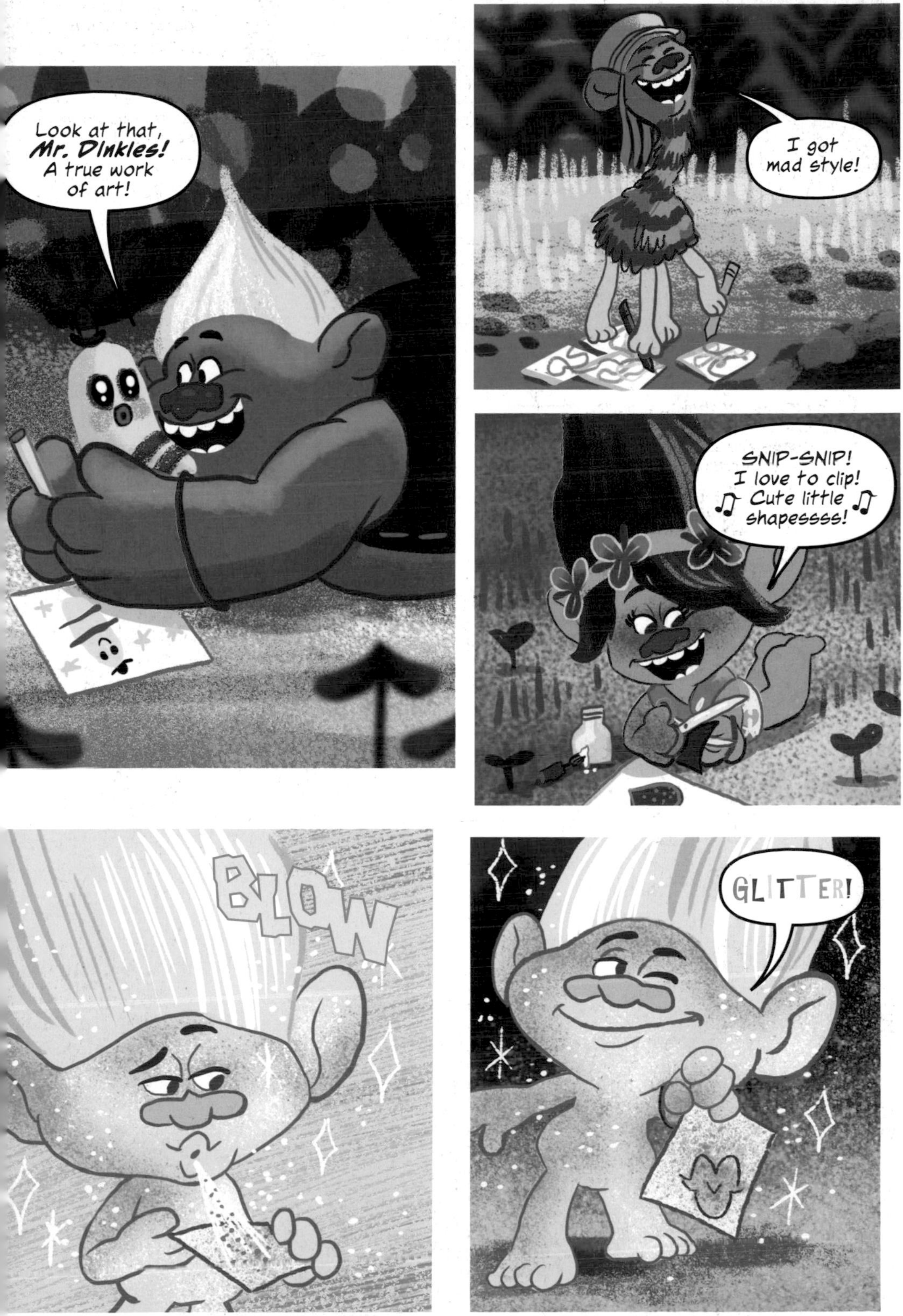
Look at that, ***Mr. Dinkles!*** A true work of art!
I got mad style!
SNIP-SNIP! I love to clip! ♫ Cute little ♫ shapessss!
BLOW
GLITTER!

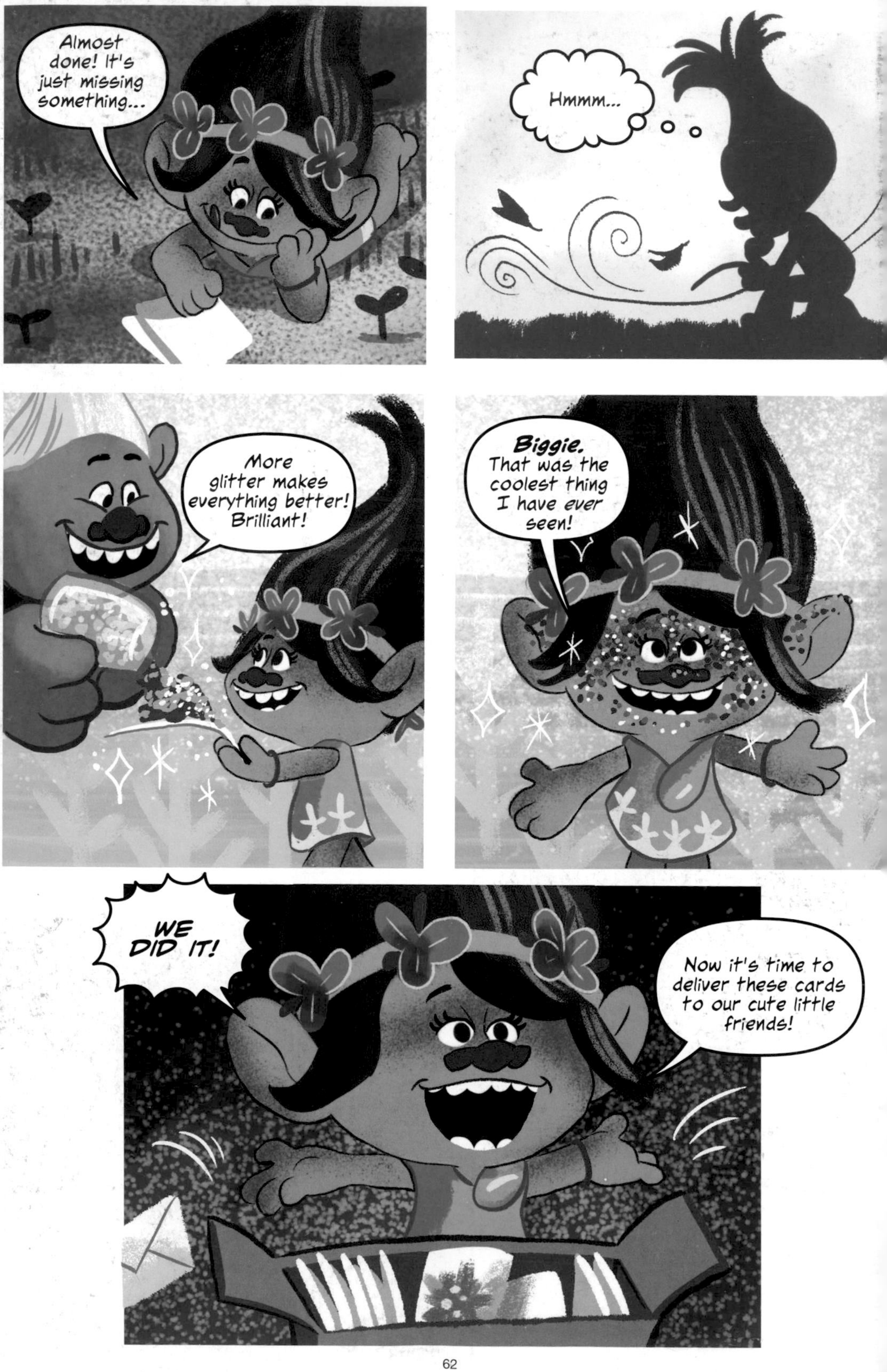

Almost done! It's just missing something...
Hmmm...
More glitter makes everything better! Brilliant!
Biggie. That was the coolest thing I have ever seen!
WE DID IT!
Now it's time to deliver these cards to our cute little friends!

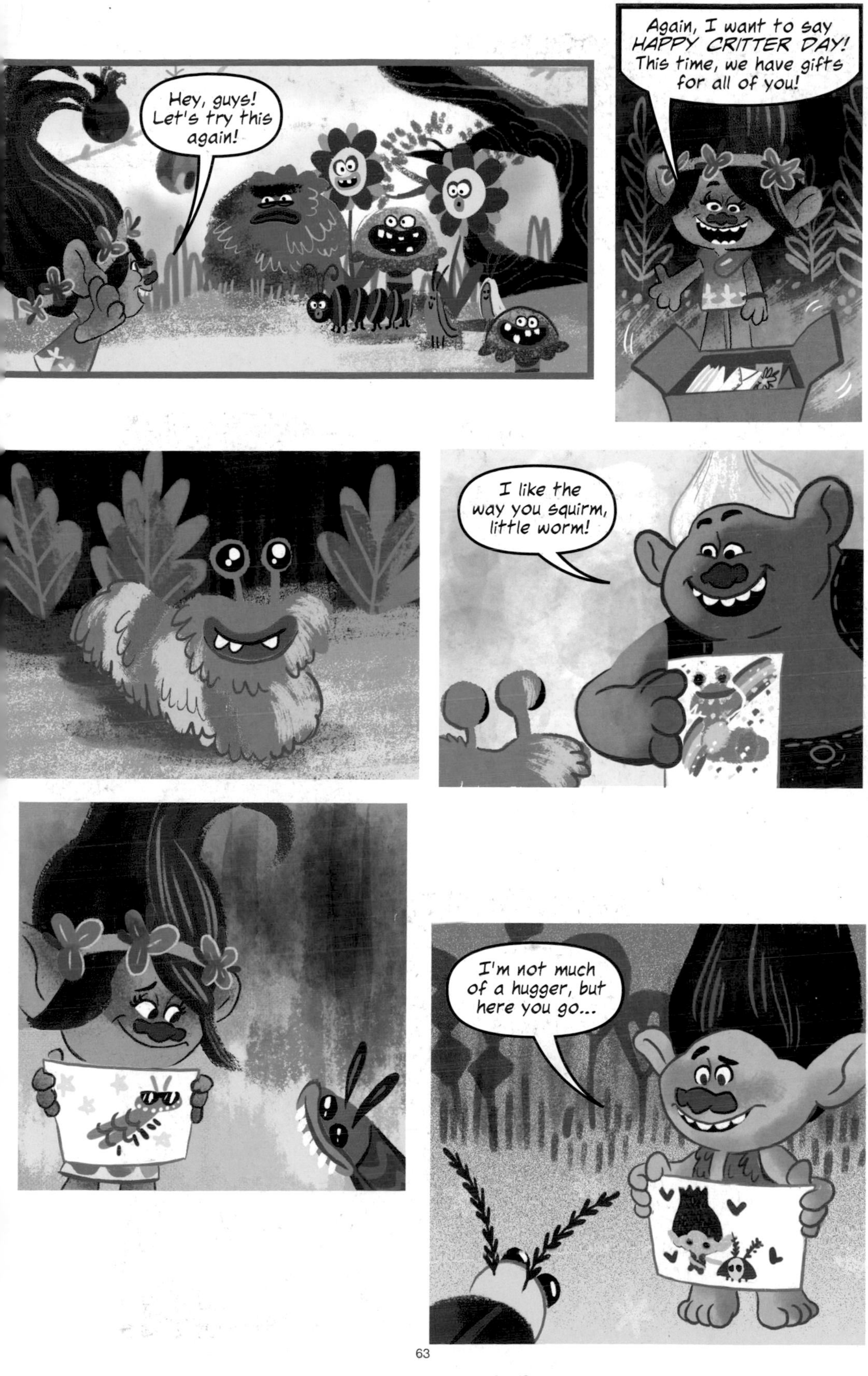
Hey, guys! Let's try this again!
Again, I want to say HAPPY CRITTER DAY! This time, we have gifts for all of you!
I like the way you squirm, little worm!
I'm not much of a hugger, but here you go...

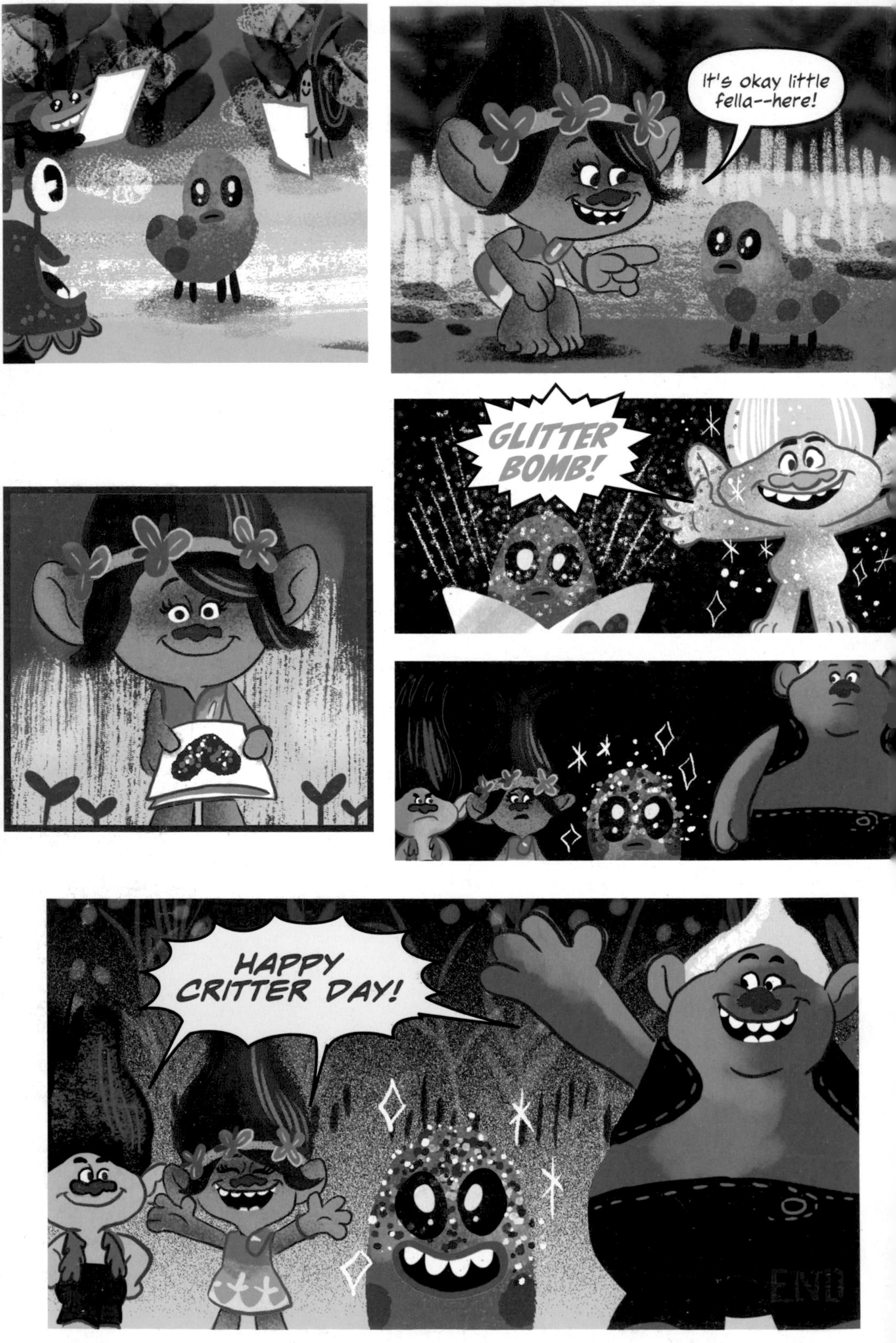
It's okay little fella--here!
GLITTER BOMB!
HAPPY CRITTER DAY!
END